"What did I do wrong, the bag and trying to keep up with her with my arms completely full of purchases.

"Nothing, Mr. McTavish, not one thing."

"Then wait—" She was fast leaving me, and I was too loaded down to run far after her.

"No, I've already wasted an hour on you. I've got to head for home," she said over her shoulder. "You have your getup. Now go away."

"Miss Rice!" I shouted. There was one last chance of my stopping her. "Miss Rice!" She turned in the seat to look at me with a frown.

"If you don't stop this minute, I'm going back there and tell everyone in that store you and I are engaged!"

Stout stood up to saw her horses to a stop. She whirled around to see if anyone heard me, her face turning bright crimson. Standing up in the wagon, hands on her hips, she looked at me defiantly over the tarped load.

"You wouldn't dare."

"Oh, I would, Miss Rice," I promised as I hurried to toss my valise, new clothes, and bedroll in the wagon box and then climbed up on the seat. "Oh, I'd tell them that in a very swift moment if you left me. . . ."

PRAISE FOR *FROM HELL TO BREAKFAST*

"Dusty Richards has created a hilariously charming cast of characters. The Rice sisters are a lot more than beautiful; they're as tough and as bold as any man who dared to tangle with the West."

—Kathleen O'Neal Gear and W. Michael Gear,
authors of the bestselling *People of the River*

Books by Dusty Richards

By the Cut of Your Clothes*
From Hell to Breakfast*
Noble's Way

*Published by POCKET BOOKS

BY THE CUT OF YOUR CLOTHES

DUSTY RICHARDS

POCKET BOOKS

New York   London   Toronto   Sydney   Tokyo   Singapore

This book is a work of fiction. Names, characters, places and
incidents are products of the author's imagination or are used
fictitiously. Any resemblance to actual events or locales or persons,
living or dead, is entirely coincidental.

An *Original* Publication of POCKET BOOKS

POCKET BOOKS, a division of Simon & Schuster Inc.
1230 Avenue of the Americas, New York, NY 10020

Copyright © 1995 by Dusty Richards

ISBN: 0-671-87242-7

First Pocket Books printing February 1995

10 9 8 7 6 5 4 3 2 1

POCKET and colophon are registered trademarks of
Simon & Schuster Inc.

Cover art by Tim Tanner

Printed in the U.S.A.

I dedicate this book to my dad, John, for his close call one time with an Arizona bear near Perkinsville, and to my mother, Jean, who read the Will James books to me as a boy. I also dedicate this book to Tommy Due, who knows all about capturing trophy trout in the Arkansas White River, to my writer friends, and to my wife, Pat, who believed all along there was a place for my tales of the Old West. Gracias, amigos.

BY THE CUT OF YOUR CLOTHES

CHAPTER

1

My vision was blurred, yet I noted that two dusty pointed-toe boots were parked in front of me when I rose to my all fours. Spurs, cord pants, with the hem of a riding skirt over them, forced me to blink. As I straightened, I saw she carried a gun in a holster and held her hands on her hips, holding open the linen duster coat that so many drovers wore in the West. The brim of her cowboy hat was bent down in the front, and a leather thong under her chin held the headgear on. She was a large girl, tall as I and broad built, but a very lovely young lady, perhaps near twenty years old, I surmised. When she started to speak I wanted to smile at her beauty.

"Are you going to whip that bully or do I have to?" she asked.

I must have stared at her ever so briefly before I recalled why I'd been on the ground. A tall bearded man had struck me on the jaw during an altercation.

Suddenly, I heard the roar of my adversary, which hurt my eardrums. My attention shifted from the pretty gal. Slowly I rose to my feet, sizing up the situation. A great ham of a hand clamped my shoulder and roughly spun me around to face this ugly fellow with bloodshot eyes, matted beard, and yellow teeth that looked near rotted.

He drew back his fist with a deep-throated growl. There is an old saying about you hit me once with a surprise punch, so be it, but never again. I dodged the man's powerhouse swing, ducked under his intended force, and drove my fist like a freight train into his belly. The air was forced from his body, and he gave out a long "ah" sound. My next blow struck the side of his rock-hard head and spun him sideways. I delivered the last punch with a haymaker swing that spilled him flat on his back in the dust.

"Have you had enough?" I demanded of my adversary.

He waved a hand in defeat, and I accepted his surrender, turning to look for the handsome woman. I clapped my hands together to rid them of the dirt. Then I smiled at the young lady's approach. She handed me my bowler, which I'd lost in the melee.

"My name is Locke McTavish," I offered, "and I'm most grateful for your encouragement during my altercation."

"Stout Rice," she said, and stuck out her hand like a man.

I was taken aback but accepted her long fingers and firm grasp.

"I'm not sure about my encouragement. You didn't need much help to finish that bully off," she said.

"Did you know either party?" I asked.

"Nope, but that big guy was sure kicking hell out of the other one and him down when I stopped my team. I decided someone needed to do something about it. That's when I saw you set down your bag and step in. He hit you a good one the first time. Are you sure you're all right?"

I rubbed my tender jaw gingerly. "Yes, ma'am, I certainly agree the situation was deplorable for the lesser man when I arrived."

She smiled with a shake of her head. "Where do you come from talking like that?"

"Illinois, but I'm making my home here in the West."

"You are? What are you going to do out here?"

"Ranch," I said, not completely certain why she was so amused at me and my speech.

"Have you ever ranched before?"

"No, but I have farmed."

Miss Rice was openly laughing at my expense, I decided. "Mr. McTavish, if you've never ranched before, how can you expect to just start ranching?"

"Can you show me how?" I asked, a little indignant that such a lovely girl thought I was just a jester. I was very serious about ranching in the area.

She looked me over from head to toe with her steel blue eyes and then shook her head. "I don't think I have that much time. Besides, I need to get back home with the supplies in this wagon."

"I'm not in any hurry. Perhaps I could assist you, and you could tell me all about ranching while we drove?" I asked, not anxious for this frontier woman to escape me. I kept looking at her blue eyes. They

3

were alive with mischief and, yes, even some was directed at me, but never in my twenty-eight years had I ever seen such a woman who so totally fascinated me.

"I'm taking these supplies to our ranch. You don't understand. It's a hundred miles from here."

"Miss Rice, I'm a proper gentleman."

She shook her head to dismiss my concern about the matter of her reputation and acted ready to climb in the wagon seat. "I'm not afraid of you. It's just a long ways to drive a wagon, and you'll end up a long ways from Flagstaff when you get there."

"No matter, I'd be ready in a jiffy. All I have to do is buy a few items and I'll be ready to travel."

"Have to buy what?" she asked with a frown.

"Clothing, of course. In Rome during Caesar's time they wore togas. There is a saying, 'When in Rome do as the Romans do.' My suit and spats are not the common mode of dress here in Flagstaff, I can see."

"I've never been to Rome, but sure you could use some different duds." She almost laughed again, no doubt at my attire.

"Good." I felt pleased she had softened her attitude toward me.

From the corner of my eye I watched the bully sluggishly drag himself up and go hobbling off, making angry side glances back at me. The smaller man who had been the point of the attack had vanished when my fight started. I knew neither man. As I took in the splendid snow-capped San Francisco peaks above Flagstaff, I drew my first deep breath of truly rarified mountain air since stepping from the train.

"Lovely here," I said, admiring the traffic and

picking up my luggage. "Miss Rice, would you direct me to the nearest haberdashery?"

She frowned and shook her head. "I ain't sure they got one here in Flagstaff."

"A clothing store?"

"Oh well, Babbett Brothers has everything you'll need if you intend to dress like the folks around here do."

"Then would you please show me to these Babbett Brothers?"

Miss Rice climbed on the wheel and stepped in the wagon box. "Throw your stuff in and get on. I'm not exactly certain why I'm doing all this, but I'll take you to Babbett's, and later we can talk about you going to the ranch with me."

"I can do my share. I am an able cook, woodsman, and can shoot well." I hoped I didn't sound like a braggart but I wanted her to know from the first that I was a trained, capable person in the wilderness. Jerome Claus had instructed me on the numerous things I'd need to know on the frontier. Jerome had worked for the Hudson Bay Company for several years, so with his experience, he prepared me for the lack of conveniences out in the territory.

"What have you ever shot?" she asked as I found myself seated very close to her on the spring seat.

"What caliber?" I asked.

"Caliber? Hell, do you even have a gun with you?"

I frowned at her words. "No, I wasn't certain of the need for one."

"Mister, if you're going to ranch—Lord, even live out here, you better go to carrying a hawg leg on your hip. Fists won't always work as the way to handle some of this trash you'll run into." Miss Rice never looked in my direction. She unwrapped the reins, kicked the brake off, and clucked to the big horses.

"A hawg leg?" I asked, as the wagon began to move, unfamiliar with her terminology.

"A Colt pistol. They sell them everywhere for eighteen bucks, single action, so you ain't half liable to shoot your foot off jerking it out and pulling the trigger at the same time."

"What caliber?"

"A forty-four will fit in a Winchester rifle as well. Then you ain't packing two kinds of ammo."

"This weapon of yours—ah, your hawg leg?" I glanced down between us at the gun she wore.

"It's a thirty-two, big enough for anything bothers me." She reached down and adjusted it. Then she took up the reins in each hand and drove the horses across the double railroad tracks. That was the Santa Fe railroad I had arrived on, their coach service that went on to Los Angeles. I had no more than debarked the Pullman car when I spotted this one man attacking the other and met Stout Rice—certainly a flower in the rather raw city of Flagstaff, Arizona Territory. At this time in the early 1880s much of this region, according to newspaper reports, harbored savage Indians, outlaws, and guerrillas. So my discover of such beauty as Stout Rice in this wild land was indeed my good fortune.

By my observations I decided that Flagstaff supported many logging businesses. The air smelled of sawn wood, stacks of pine lumber were all about. Oxen teams hauled in loads of large logs, and commerce in the city looked rather brisk, with many freighters threading around parked drays with loads of goods.

The Indians in the streets held my interest the most. They wore feathers in their hair, wrapped themselves in colorful blankets, and walked about with an aloof air as though they were above the white man's business and trade. Their women wore many layered skirts and much silver jewelry that glistened in the diamond-clear air—brilliant skies save for some smoke I suspected came from millwright works and boilers to power sawmills. Still, there was a vastness in Arizona one never felt in Illinois. I experienced the feeling the moment I arrived, wider spans of elbow-room for everyone, immediate freedom from fences and close by neighbors. Even the mountain, the tallest one above the town, seemed to be untouched, the steep snowy slopes untracked. I drew in another deep breath and looked over at Stout Rice. How did such a lovely girl ever get such an unusual name? I promised myself to ask her when we were better acquainted. It might prove to be a family name or even her grandmother's, and I didn't wish to make her mad thinking I was making fun of her given name.

"This is it, Mr. McTavish." Miss Rice reined in the team before the large store. I could read Babbett Brothers on the sign. The posted list of items they stocked looked rather complete, as she had promised.

"You will get down and help me make these choices?" I asked as I stepped on the wagon wheel to dismount. "I am, as the man on the train called me, a pilgrim, and this is my first step on Plymouth Rock."

"Do I look like some East Coast Indian?" she asked, staring straight ahead, making no effort to tie up the lines on the brake handle. She pushed her hat back so it slipped from her head and rested on her shoulders, the leather string caught at her throat. This device, I thought, would be highly desirable riding a fast horse or buffeting a great windstorm as the West reportedly suffered from time to time.

"No," I said quickly, "but you do understand, I wish to attire myself in the manner and mode in which people in this region dress. I would appreciate your expertise in the matter."

"Gods, you talk so strange at times," she said, tying up the lines and moving to get down, "I can't even believe you come from America. Does everyone in Illinois talk like you do?"

"Certainly educated people do, though there are some rural people in southern Illinois that drawl rather like southerners."

On the porch I stopped to let Miss Rice go inside the store first and drew a steely look from her, but she went ahead.

"I don't," she said, then she lowered her voice, "want these clerks in here to know that I'm here with you."

"Why not?" I whispered.

"I have my reasons." Miss Rice looked across the room at some bolts of material. "When you try on something I'll nod if it looks okay. That is, if it looks like something folks around here would wear. Act like you're being polite to me and we aren't together—go on!"

Whatever her reason for disowning me at this point I was not certain. I was grateful she had not totally abandoned me, for I did plan to accompany her to her ranch and use the time in travel to convince her I might be a pilgrim, but at the very least a resourceful one.

"Good day, sir," a young clerk said. "My name's Jed."

"Good day, yourself. My name's McTavish, and I've just arrived in your metropolis and I'm sorely in need of adequate clothing."

"For what, sir?"

"For ranching. I need the proper attire for ranching. Do you know what I mean, Jed?"

"Sheep or cattle?"

"Does it make a lot of difference?" I asked, and looked for Stout to help me, but she was out of sight. Damn, she was letting me make a large ass out of myself with this young man. "Jed, I want to look like a cowboy when I leave here. I mean a tough cowboy, one that no one will mess with."

"You'll need a pair of cord pants to start," Jed said, looking me over for size. "Here." He chose a pair from a stack. "They'll shrink, so they'll be a little big at first. You'll need galluses to hold them up. I've got the shirts that have a button-up bib front or a collarless model that you can add a celluloid collar to when you dress up."

"What do cowboys dress up for?" I asked, wondering whatever happened out there requiring formal dress.

"Dances and funerals, I guess. Myself, I've never been one, but I have sold a lot of clothes to ah— cowboys working around here."

9

"Very good. I like the blue shirt with the bib, it looks much like the one the army wears." I held the shirt before me and imagined what it looked like on. I hoped Miss Rice could see it.

"There's a mirror over there," the young man pointed out.

"Very good," I said, and went across the room to the framed looking glass and held up the shirt. From behind the bolts of calico I saw Miss Rice nod in approval.

"You'll need a vest," the young man said, squeezing his jaw and studying me when I returned.

"What kind?"

"Best one I've got is what only a few cowboys can afford. It's a kidskin vest with hammered silver buttons."

"How much?"

"Fifteen bucks to you with all you're buying here." He took one from the rack, and I slipped my arms into it. Perfect fit. It did look very western, but then I saw Miss Rice across the room turning over dry goods and ruefully shaking her head. What was wrong with her? The vest looked nice. I liked the vest. Why didn't she like it? To hell with her, I thought, I was taking it anyway.

"I need boots and a hat too," I reminded the young man.

"We got a new shipment of Kansas-made boots, some of the best ones made, but they also aren't cheap."

"Kansas boots?" What did the lad mean?

"Means they come in sizes to fit, sir. You don't have to stuff them full of newspaper to keep them on your feet like you used to have to do with store-bought boots."

Jed found a pair the right size in the mountain of boxes. I stomped around the store in my Coffeyville boots—they did feel good. They cost thirty dollars, and the spurs I strapped on them were five. The total was adding up fast.

"Oh yes," I said, "a hat and a gun, and I'll be off."

"You'll need a duster for the elements, won't you?" the clerk asked, and I saw Miss Rice bob her head in agreement at a distance. "And a bedroll, too, if you're going out there." Jed tossed his head to mean the rest of Arizona, I guessed.

"Yes, I will," I agreed.

The sum total of my purchases came to over one hundred and fifty dollars, a figure I had no regrets over. I knew when I dressed in the outfit I would be less likely to be taken as an outsider. I paid the young man and thanked him. With my new wardrobe, gun, hat, and bedroll under my arm, I went outside to look for Stout.

I'd heard another clerk say good-bye to her. My heart was pounding in my chest. I stood on the store porch and searched the street. The wagon was a half block away when I stepped off the porch. I ran pell-mell through the traffic to catch her.

"Aren't you forgetting something?" I asked, out of breath from keeping up with the wagon. She looked ahead very steel-eyed, never offered to stop, and kept her attention centered on the street crowded with rigs and which way to swing her team to avoid the obstacles.

"Say, don't you remember me?" I demanded.

"You want your bag? Sorry, I forgot I had it." She reined in the horses and reached for my valise. "Here!" She tossed it down.

"What did I do wrong?" I asked, snatching up the bag and trying to keep up with her with my arms completely full of bag and purchases.

"Nothing, Mr. McTavish, not one thing."

"Then wait, Miss Rice—" She was fast leaving me, and I was too loaded down to run far after her.

"No, I've already wasted an hour on you. I've got to head for home," she said over her shoulder. "You have your getup. Now go away."

"Miss Rice!" I shouted. There was one last chance of my stopping her. "Miss Rice!" She turned in the seat to look back at me with a frown.

"If you don't stop this minute, I'm going back there and tell everyone in that store you and I are engaged!"

Miss Rice stood up to saw her horses to a stop. She whirled around to see if anyone heard me. A grizzly old man leading a burro past nodded at me. A shovel and gold pan stuck out of the packs, so I concluded he was a miner.

"I'd tell her that myself," the miner said to me, "if it would do any damn good, sonny. Boy, she's a fiery one, ain't she? Say, I liked big strapping girls in my younger days meself. Stay in there, lad." He left chuckling out of his toothless mouth.

Miss Rice's face turned crimson. Standing up in the wagon, hands on her hips, she defiantly looked at me over the tarped load.

"You wouldn't dare?"

"Oh, I would, Miss Rice," I promised as I hurried to toss my valise, new clothes, and bedroll in the wagon box, then climbed up on the seat. "Oh, I'd tell them that in a very swift moment if you left me."

Wordless, Miss Rice sat down heavily beside me. I wasn't sure why telling those clerks such a lie was the worst thing I could do to that lovely woman, but my ploy had worked, and I was again seated beside her. Miss Rice very deliberately untwisted the reins, kicked the brake off, and clucked to the team. To my relief, we were soon headed south for the tracks, and, I supposed, to her ranch.

CHAPTER
2

Miss Rice drove the team and I studied the countryside. I figured when that girl wanted to talk to me she would. There was lots of open grassland and beyond that, pine forests. We passed some small places, farms I guessed, but they looked awfully dry to me, the grass all brown and very short. She'd get over being mad at me for blackmailing her into taking me along on the spring seat beside her. I was disappointed by the patches of corn. They looked pitiful and stunted, especially after being accustomed to looking at Illinois crops.

"You look pretty damn silly tromping around in those boots and spurs and wearing that green checkered suit," Miss Rice said, speaking for the first time since we had left Flagstaff.

I smiled to myself. I was grateful to be seated beside her and not left to my own devices in town. "I'll change at the first stop we make. Why didn't you like that vest I bought?"

"Because you look like a damn gun slick in it."

"A what?" Lord, she had words I'd never heard of before.

"Aw, one of those high-priced vinegaroons would wear a vest like that. Gunslingers, you know, that the big outfits hire to crowd the small ranchers out."

I nodded but I didn't have a half notion what a vinegaroon was. And "crowd" meant people to me. I folded my arms on my chest and sat on the seat so as not to touch her and have her think I was being too familiar or disrespectful. With the lurch of the wagon and all, our bottoms were wedged very familiarlike against each other on the narrow seat. I enjoyed the contact, but I didn't want her to think I was some kind of a perverted person.

"Where will we camp tonight?" I asked.

She gave me a cold look, then clucked for the team to jog. "I'm not sure. We got too late a start to make Mormon Lake, so I reckon we'll camp along the road."

"Fine." I really meant thanks, for she was talking of 'we' again. Maybe she wouldn't haul off and leave me behind first chance she got. I hoped that before we reached her ranch we'd be on much friendlier terms. I felt certain our relationship would improve as time wore on.

We rested the horses at midday. Miss Rice served dried crackers and cheese for lunch. We washed them down with stale water from a barrel on the side of the wagon. Not a three-course meal, but I was pleased.

After four days on the train and the depot food I'd eaten, her cheese and crackers was one rung above the previous menu.

"We need to kill a cottontail rabbit this afternoon," she said. "Otherwise we'll eat fatback with our beans."

"Fine," I agreed, finished eating, and wiped my mouth on the handkerchief from my coat pocket.

"If you want to change your clothes, we've got time," she said.

I looked around. There wasn't a suitable thicket in sight to change behind. The nearest woods were well over a quarter mile away. "If you don't mind, I'll wait till evening," I said.

"Suit yourself, but I'd hate to meet anyone I know and them see you perched up on that seat with me like a big green checkered buzzard."

She seemingly didn't like my clothing, so I decided it would be best to oblige her. "I'll change on the other side of the wagon," I said.

"You can change on this side, I ain't going to watch," she said, and walked away.

I considered her as she went off. Hat hung on her back, her soft light brown hair had highlights of gold through it. Cut very short, it was as attractive as the rest of her. I turned my attention to undressing since she was leaving. From behind the wagon, I soon stripped to my underwear, then peeked over the top of the canvas to see where she went. Miss Rice must have gone into a ravine, for she was not in view. I hurriedly pulled on the new stiff pants, took on the shirt, hooked on the galluses, and had them up by the time I saw her slowly returning studying the ground as she came.

I tried on the wide-brim hat and was finished buttoning the vest when she walked around me inspectively. I took the stiff new holster and buckled it on, then shoved the oily Colt inside.

"Well?" I asked since she had not said a word.

"You drive," she said, and caught my hat by the brim and flipped it off my head. "This hat of yours needs a lot of fixing."

My eyes flew wide open when she opened the lid on the water barrel and doused my brand new Philadelphia hat down inside it with vengeance. She pulled it out dripping water. It looked like a drowned cat fished out of a creek. Half sick, I climbed up on the seat in a state of numb shock. My brand-new hat looked like a dishrag. I undid the lines and then offered her a hand up, for she seemed totally engrossed in doing something to my wet new hat.

Miss Rice sat down beside me, her full attention devoted to my soggy headwear. She looked at it like she was sizing it, then used the side of her hand to dent the crown from top to bottom. The crease looked like a canyon in the side of the San Francisco Mountains to me. Then she took the sides of the brim and rolled them like a newspaper.

"Are we going to sit here all day or can't you drive?" she asked, sort of impatient we weren't rolling. She held the hat up and studied her work as the big team shouldered the wagon and we began moving.

"A hat's special. Tells you a lot about a man when I see him riding up. Second, it needs to be his property and not look like any ranny, especially one he don't like. Why, folks might think you're kinfolks if your hats look alike. You savvy all this?" she asked.

"Most of it," I said, and smiled. The horses were mighty good ones. I'd almost forgotten the notion of handling a fine pair of animals.

"Hold still," she said, balancing herself with her hand on my shoulder. She dragged out a canvas bag from behind the seat, swung it up front, and opened the drawstring. "You'll need one of these sacks if you're going to cowboy much."

"What is it called?" I asked.

"A war bag I guess. I call them that. The drawstrings can hang off a saddle horn, brush won't chew them up, and they'll shed rain so you can store a lot of your things in one. Cowboy luggage is all."

She rummaged inside the sack and came out with a long leather string. I drove and watched her make holes in two rose-shaped pieces of leather, then she threaded the string through them. Then she awed two holes in my new hat to thread through the leather string. I could see her purpose and felt grateful my teacher was doing all this. I wouldn't lose my hat with a string to hold it on.

I had to shift the holster and pistol back on my side. She frowned at me. "Did you ever bother to load that gun?"

My face grew red. I shook my head at the omission and kept on driving. Rather stupid to carry a gun and not have it loaded. Oh my, I had a lot to learn to live in this country. One thing was for certain, I had better catch on quickly, or she'd give up on me as being too dumb. It was going to be an interesting few days we'd spend together. I must admit I looked forward to the time with an eagerness that made my skin tingle.

We made a camp beside a stone mortar water tank

fed by a windmill. The old homestead cabin was fallen in and so was the small chicken house, the roof rotted down like the house. I unhitched the team and she helped me unharness them. I used a rag to rub down their shoulders, making certain they had no collar marks that would hurt them.

"You do know horses, don't you?" she asked with a tone of appreciation. "Can you start a fire?"

"Yes, I can do that too," I said proudly. I'd finally done something in our first ten hours together to draw her praise.

"I'm going to shoot a cottontail for supper if you can make a fire and start the beans to cooking."

"I'll manage." I watched her swinging walk out through the sage and low grass. Stout Rice was certainly nice to look after.

I chopped up some kindling and started at the pop of her pistol, then I heard another shot and rose up to look for her, but she was out of sight. She'd probably missed. Beans would be enough for me. I drew in a deep breath of the resin clean air. It was great land, a little dry, but I liked it. We'd passed a half dozen wagons headed for Flagstaff—some freighters and a few ranchers that nodded at us—no one that she knew.

Miss Rice came back holding her prize high as I finished putting the beans in the iron kettle. Two rabbits, and I noticed both were shot in the head. If this was my lesson in her marksmanship, then I was impressed, even at close range. A rabbit never was in close range for very long. That was real shooting. I wouldn't try to compete with her.

While the rabbits and beans cooked, she told me

about her two younger sisters at home. Erv was eighteen and Tate, fifteen, and their father, Ewell. They ran cattle in a place called the North Cut. I listened, and she told me about their mother dying when they were very little and how her father raised the sisters, by her own admission, a little on the rough side.

"Aw," Miss Rice said, throwing a handful of small twigs on the fire to blaze, "he just showed us how to take care of ourselves."

"Yes, I can see that."

"Well, last fall, my brother-in-law to be, H. B. Bentley, along with me and my sisters broke up the largest rustling ring in this territory."

"How?"

"That's a whole 'nother story," she said. "Where did you get all your highbrow learning?"

I blinked at her. What did she mean by highbrow?

"Shush, someone's coming," she said, and rose to her feet, listening to the night. I heard the soft fall of hooves and noticed her hand was on her gun handle.

"Something wrong?" I asked.

"Can't see who it is," she whispered back.

"Hello the camp! I'm coming in," the man said.

I took her lead and stepped apart from her until we learned the man's identity.

"Howdy, smelled your fire and thought I'd stop a moment," he said, dismounting the blaze-faced horse. "My name's Floyd Tillman, I'm a U.S. deputy marshal." He drew back his vest and the silver star shone in the night. "That you, Miss Rice? I thought that was you two. You're the one got off the train and handled that big guy they were talking about."

"Locke McTavish," I said, extending my hand to the man, "You know Miss Stout Rice, sir?

"I know Stout. Well, I've met her before." He nodded and she returned the salutation.

Tillman looked like his whole upper lip was crowded with mustache, the corners dropped in a fine twist like longhorn cattle horns. The man stood a head shorter than me. He looked as bowlegged as any man I'd ever seen—no doubt lots of horse-riding made one's legs bend in a fashion to fit the horse's sides.

"Have some food with us, Marshal," Miss Rice offered.

"I would indeed. Did you know those two men you had the fight with?" Tillman asked me as she fixed his plate.

I shook my head. "Never saw them before. This is my first time in this country. I got off the Santa Fe coach and there they were, the big one kicking the small one."

"You never saw them leave? Which way they went?"

"No sir, why?"

"I was told it was Serval Dingus and Mink Seawell."

"Who are they?" I asked as Stout handed him a tin plate of steaming beans and rabbit parts.

"Killers, robbers, and worse, I'm afraid. They've done some terrible crimes against Indians. They broke out of Yuma Prison about three weeks ago and have been the scourge of the earth ever since."

"Why were they fighting each other then? That big guy had the little one down and was kicking him hard when I saw them."

"Bad enough," Stout said, "I'd have stopped to break it up if Locke here hadn't done something."

"Guess they got awful drunk and were arguing over something between themselves. They were really in the chips earlier in a bar. Told the bartender a grisly tale about assaulting some Indian girls down on the Gila River a week ago." Tillman shook his head as if he'd rather not say more. "They also robbed a stage near the Hassayampa River, shot an army payroll officer to death. There are some witnesses to that crime. That's what I want them for."

"Did they ride out of Flagstaff?" Miss Rice asked.

"Yes, and I have reason to believe they're somewhere ahead of you two."

Tillman settled down to eat his food. I peered out in the darkness and wondered where those two killers had gone. I tried to remember the big one's distinguishing features—his shaggy, matted beard and rotten teeth. I wouldn't forget him soon. The small man had run away as soon as I pulled the big man off him, so I couldn't remember much about him. I'd been that close to real frontier killers, true outlaws, and had not been killed—too narrow an escape for a pilgrim. Serval Dingus was the big one, I supposed, and Mink Seawell, the small one. Mink fit him, for he was like a weasel the way he fled so quickly. I barely could recall a feature about the man.

"You two better keep your hog legs handy going home. There's good odds those two may be in New Mexico already, but don't take no chances."

We both nodded in agreement.

The lawman wiped his mouth on the kerchief from around his neck and set the plate down.

"Good food. Thanks. I'm riding on tonight."

"You're welcome to sleep here till morning," Miss Rice said.

"Thanks anyway, Miss Rice, but I'd like to be close to their camp come sunup if I can," Tillman said, resetting the flat-brimmed hat on his head. His headgear had an individual look, all right, the block on top was dimpled on four sides. I was learning more about western hats.

"Miss Stout, if I ever get back to that schoolhouse up there in your country, would you save a waltz for me?"

"The Pecan Schoolhouse—yes I would." I swear Stout was blushing and had to turn away to keep us from seeing it.

"Young man, you're in mighty good company with Miss Stout here, and she's a right smart dancer too. Good evening, *mi amigos.*" He gathered up his reins, booted his horse in the jaw to make him stop eating grass and raise his head, then he mounted and rode out into the starlit night.

We stood in silence and listened to his horse's hoofbeats vanish in the night.

"You kinda soft on him?" I asked.

"That's none of your business."

"I reckon it ain't," I agreed, and sat back down wondering more about those killers. Besides, Miss Rice had her own life to lead—though I considered the man near old enough to be her father. Some women liked older men. So there was competition in the field for her. Fine, but I ought to be able to outshine an old man like Tillman.

"You dance much?" I asked.

She shook her head and peered into the fire. "I just had a strange sad feeling a few minutes ago. When he asked me about the dance."

"What kinda feeling?" I asked.

"I'm not sure, but it wasn't a good one, like I knew something bad was going to happen and couldn't speak about it."

"Should we post guards? Take turns?" I asked.

"No, but we better sleep out in the sage and not near the wagon, so if anyone creeps up they won't spot us before we hear them."

It was a splendid idea. I only wished I'd thought of doing it before she did.

My bedroll outfit smelled new when I rolled it out and crawled inside it. I finally shut my eyes —my freshly loaded Colt inside the blankets just in case. I wondered about Stout and her suitors. She must have several. My eyes finally closed and I slept.

"Time to roll out," she said, nudging me with her boot toe.

I half jumped out of my blankets and searched around. It was still dark and very cold. Relieved that nothing seemed amiss at the moment, I rubbed the back of my neck. At least I hadn't slept till noon, and she hadn't driven off without me.

"Time to get going if we're ever to get to my place," she said.

I agreed, took the steaming coffee cup she handed me, and stood up in a stupor. How long she had been up making the fire and coffee, I had no idea. I had passed one test of my own—I slept well on the ground, so I might yet survive in this bedless land. She led the horses around to put on the harness, and I jumped in to help her.

"Where'll we camp tonight?" I asked.

"Mormon Lake this afternoon, I guess."

"Good. I wonder where Tillman is by now? Is he kind of your boyfriend?"

"What?" she asked, making a terrible face. Miss Rice elbowed me aside impatiently and reset the harness on my horse as if I'd done it wrong. I wasn't about to redo it after she did that.

"Is that U.S. marshal one of your suitors?" I asked.

"Lord, no." She shook her head. "He's just some old man who comes and asks me or one of my sisters to dance up there."

"Sounds exciting."

She considered me for a long moment, then shook her head in disapproval and finished buckling up the harness with a few sharp tugs and slaps. I knew by the set of her tight lips I was in for more silence. Miss Rice led the horses up front to hitch them without a word. I lifted the wagon tongue to help her.

Wordless, we scuffed out the fire with sand, loaded our bedding, and mounted the wagon together. She took the reins, and I sat on the seat again beside a woman as indifferent as you could be sitting wedged in a spring seat with a fellow my size.

The sun greeted us as we drove southeastward. First, a blazing horizon, then the fiery ball rose above the forested hills. The spectacular phases of this new land impressed me as we rocked along on the seat. My hip pressed tight against Stout Rice's—in silence. I wasn't learning much about ranching but I wasn't complaining either since I'd learned that old Marshal Tillman wasn't competing with me for her favor.

CHAPTER

3

I sat on the wagon seat beside her, awed at my first view of the emerald gem called Mormon Lake. The small lake looked like an oasis to me. A few pines grew to the irregular smooth shoreline, but the rest of the lake was bordered by the grassy plains. The lake had a placid surface this late afternoon except for the dimples of fish feeding on the top water. I wished for a fishing rod. The setting so amazed me, especially after nearly two days of dust, I could scarcely believe my eyes.

"She's a grand body of water, isn't she?" I asked.

"Nice place, biggest lake around I know of," Miss Rice said. "Kind of a treat to camp here, I guess."

"Oh, it looks so peaceful and inviting," I said, stretching my arms over my head.

"Hey, can you unhook these horses and water them by yourself all right?" she asked, nudging me into awareness with her elbow.

"Certainly, Miss Rice," I said to get a little revenge for her silence most of the day.

"You better go to calling me Stout." She gave me a wry look. "I'll be back in a little while. I'm going to take a bath if you can handle the chores here."

"Stout?" I asked as I climbed down after her. She already had a large sack towel slung over her shoulder.

"Yes?" she asked blinking her eyes.

"You have yourself a nice bath."

The set to her eye looked like she questioned my motives for a moment. "I will, Locke. You can take one while I cook supper if you want to."

"Thanks, thanks very much," I said, grateful for her concessions and for talking to me at last. "I'll do that."

Once the team of horses was unhitched, I walked them to the lake. There was no sign of her when the horses drank deeply, though I expected she went to some cove to bathe. With the horses finally hobbled and out to graze, I chopped wood and busied myself preparing for a fire.

Whistling, Stout returned drying her hair. I smiled at her approach. She wore her riding skirt, her britches over her arm. Stout looked as fresh as a summer peach. At times I couldn't believe my good fortune meeting her in Flagstaff.

"I'll start supper. You can take your time, it'll be ready after a while," she said. "You'll find another towel in my war bag."

"Thanks," I said, and took my leave of her to soak my skin in the inviting water. I chose a spot out of view behind the screen of a rise and with no one in sight. I unbuckled my gun belt and dropped the holster. Soon I was down to my underwear and wading in the cold water. This magnificent land seemed hardly believable—there was no one around, nothing to bother me.

I blinked twice at the sudden approach of two riders. Where had they come from? They looked familiar as they rode up to my pile of clothing and stopped. They were a scruffy pair, but something looked familiar about them, and they both wore floppy brimmed hats.

"That's him, Serval," the short rider said, and my heart stopped. I was twenty feet from my pistol on the shore. "I told you that big heifer we watched swimming a while ago was her, the one that was with him." I didn't like Mink's chuckles. Those indecent bastards had been peeking at Stout while she bathed.

"Listen, you two thugs—" I started for shore, then stopped in my tracks when the big one, Serval, drew his pistol. There wasn't any cover standing knee-deep in water wearing your one-piece underwear.

"You listen here, Mr. Big Fighting Fellah. You come out here real slow like. I want some more of your hide." He pointed the gun hard at me to make his point.

Dang, I worried they might harm Stout. Somehow I'd survive this, but I sure didn't want her hurt for the likes of these two crooks. I was nearly to the shore. Serval stepped off his horse, holstered his gun, and then made a head-down charge at me. I sidestepped him, but he still caught me by the waist, and we spilled into the water. The sour smell of his unwashed body nearly gagged me as we struggled for a commanding grip on the other. I swallowed some fishy-tasting lake water and took a smashing blow to my face.

"Get back! Get back," Mink screamed, "and I'll shoot the sumbitch! Get the hell out of the way, Serval!"

The big man had his mind on killing me, too—with his bare hands—as we came up dripping and swinging. Water plastered Serval's hair on his face as he swung wildly at me, and I ducked around trying to keep his frame between me and that little ungrateful Mink on the bank. To think I'd even bothered to save Mink from this raging bear made me mad.

Then I heard the shot.

"Gawdamnit!" Mink shouted. "It's that damn gal of his shooting at us! Get out of there, Serval!"

The big man considered me for a long moment. Mink was swearing and shooting at her. I was beside myself, for I could see the puffs of smoke she was slinging as she ran down the slope toward them. Stay there, Stout! I wanted to shout for her to go back as Serval ran for his horse. Mink shot at her again while holding the reins of his spooked horse, then he, too, mounted and the pair fled south.

I saw Stout take the pistol in both hands and deliberately take aim after them. The gun bucked and smoke issued out the muzzle, but they were thundering away like the devil was on their heels. Damn, that girl sure looked good to me hurrying down the slope.

"Locke! Locke! Are you all right?" she cried out.

I caught her in my arms and hugged her.

"I'm fine," I said, smelling her fresh hair in my nose

and savoring her firm body against mine. "Thanks, you saved my life. I thought my goose was cooked."

"I heard those loud voices and couldn't figure out what was happening." She leaned back and looked at me with concern. "They didn't hurt you?"

"No." I released her, realizing when I glanced down that water from me had made her skirt wet. The fact I was standing there dripping wet and hugging her dressed only in my underwear made me feel a little embarrassed. We took a step or two apart.

"Wonder where they came from?" she asked. Stout was looking off to the south. Her steel eyes were slits as I pulled on my pants.

"They've been around here for a time spying on us," I said.

"Huh?" She turned to me as I tucked in my shirt.

"I hate to tell you, but Mink, the short one, said they'd been watching you swimming."

"That dirty little sneak!" Stout frowned at me. I knew if she ever got that sawed-off peeper in her gunsights, she'd make him wish he'd been watching one of those circling buzzards instead of her.

"What are we going to do?" I asked.

"I wish now I could have shot both of them," she said, still sounding mad. "But you were so close to them I couldn't risk it. I just shot in the air. She took in a deep breath of air and let it out slowly. "Well, let's go eat. I'm making some bread."

"I'm very grateful to you for saving my life," I said while fastening on my gun belt.

She looked me over from head to toe as I struggled to pull on my boots standing on one foot, no small feat with damp socks. "I guess I'm saddled with you for a while," she said, and holstered her Colt.

"Yes, ma'am," I said, pleased at her consideration. I tried not to grin, imagining what she looked like swimming in the all-together.

"Something funny?" she asked.

"Oh, no, I just never have been interrupted taking a bath before quite like this."

"You'll probably have a lot more happen to you if you live out here very long." Stout shook her head, muttered something about those lowlives spying on her, turned on her boot heels, and headed for camp.

Her sourdough bread from the Dutch oven was something I couldn't quite fully describe to cover all facets I experienced eating it. It was soft and sweet as honey, and I really had a hard time to keep from looking at her in gratitude between every bite. Sitting cross-legged side by side in the light of the fire, we enjoyed the saliva-drawing pleasures of her biscuits.

"You reckon they'll be back?" I asked.

"I'm not sure, except they damn sure didn't go to New Mexico like Marshal Tillman thought, did they? He may have gone to Winslow by now."

"I wonder where he is?"

"If I knew that, I'd sic Tillman on their trail. Those disrespectful scum spying on me makes me so damn mad." Stout folded her arms over her chest, fuming.

"Stout?"

"Yes."

"I wish I'd never told you that they'd been spying on you taking your bath, but it was the truth."

She nodded and struggled to rise. "Guess we better keep an eye out from now on, day and night. That means taking turns standing guard tonight." She brushed off her skirt. "I been thinking about you, Locke."

"Yes, ma'am?"

"You were pretty tough yourself fighting that Serval Dingus and that Mink trying to shoot you the whole time." She stood up to get something. "But I'll also bet you have a black eye in the morning."

I touched the tender socket and figured she was right. It would probably turn black and blue around my left eye. "Thanks. I'll be fine though, they didn't do much damage." I smiled as she drew a Winchester out of the box.

"Next time I'll have this gun and they won't ride off. You take the first guard shift, and I'll be up later."

"Yes, ma'am." I accepted the long rifle from her. I was almost grateful to that pair of crooks, because for the first time in two days we were conversing like normal folks. Besides that, I'd had my chance to hug her. A coyote howled out by the lake, and I felt grateful for the turn of events. Yes, I certainly did get to hug her—but the next time I met those two outlaws, I would need to do something more than fistfight with them.

Could I just shoot a man? I studied the red-white coals in the campfire as they collapsed from the log. The heat from the fire radiated on my face as the night air cooled quickly in Arizona Territory. She spread her bedroll on the ground under the wagon—close by—which made me feel important for the first time since we left Flagstaff.

That coyote out in the night yipped, then gave a mournful long cry that caused the short hair on my neck to stand stiff. Could I shoot those men? Damn, why was I so concerned about killing someone? Well, facts are facts. I'd never shot anyone before.

CHAPTER

4

As dawn was coming over the eastern horizon, we were perched side by side on the spring seat going down the dusty road. Nothing happened during the night, but we didn't get much sleep. Stout and I took turns sitting up as guards. There had been no sign of the pair of thugs. Now we were driving south by the first light. I handled the lines and Stout balanced the rifle across her lap. The country became more broken and the road much steeper in places, forcing me to brake and hold back the horses on the downgrades.

I spotted a saddled horse ahead in the road. When he raised his head from grazing, I saw his reins trailed from his bit. He was riderless, and Stout nodded that she noticed him too. I heard her cock the hammer on the Winchester. She twisted around for a once-over to be sure we weren't riding into a trap.

"See anyone?" I asked, pulling the horses down into a walk.

"No, but that horse up there looks familiar," she said twisting around again to survey more of the pine forest around us.

"I'll go check. Stay here." I stopped the team, set the brake, tied the reins, and jumped down. My heart was in my throat as I dismounted the wagon. Where was the rider? Waiting to ambush us?

Stout remained on the seat keeping guard. I felt for the Colt at my hip and decided I better have it drawn. The big team snorted softly at my back when I passed them. There hardly seemed a sound I could detect besides the wind in the pine needles as I walked cautiously toward the saddle horse. My boot soles sounded very loud crushing gravel as I moved slowly forward, speaking softly to the horse.

"See anything?" she called out.

"No," I said, capturing the animal by his bridle. He looked like any bay horse to me, and I didn't recall seeing him before. Then I spotted a pair of boots, toes pointed down under a pine tree bough.

"Stout, I think I found the owner and he's facedown over here."

"Is he dead?" she asked, climbing off the wagon.

I drew a deep breath for the strength to go in and look. Carefully, I bent aside the limbs, feeling apprehensive as I stared down at the man's bloody shirt. On my knees beside him, I gently rolled the small man over on his back. The limpness of his form told me that life had already fled his body. Worse to look at were his open eyes staring at nothing. I had a hard time bringing myself to even touch him, but I managed finally to close his eyelids.

"Badger Jones," she said, standing above me. "I wonder who shot him."

I looked back up at her. My stomach crawled like a can of worms. "I don't know. Did you know him?"

"He's a cowboy who's worked for outfits around the North Cut."

"Someone shot him in the back," I said, rising up.

"You figure Dingus and Seawell did this?" She looked hurt, standing there with the rifle in her arms.

"No way to tell. What do we need to do?" I asked, feeling close to vomiting.

"Bury him. I never heard of no kin that Badger had around here. I'll write the sheriff about this when we get home."

"You're going to write the sheriff?" I asked in disbelief.

"Yes, I'll write the Coconino County sheriff when I get home. Locke, we're two and half days from Flagstaff, and that body would be ripe by the time we got there. Besides, the sheriff wouldn't know any more than we do about the killer unless Badger left a testimony saying who killed him."

"They certainly handle the law differently out here. Is there a shovel in the wagon?" I asked, anxious to get this over as quickly as possible.

"Yes. I'll get Badger's bedroll from his horse to wrap him up in."

"Sure," I said, and headed for the wagon. No coffin for the short cowboy. Just roll him in his sleeping blankets and that was all. It sure seemed final, dying out on the frontier and someone, strangers, happening along, finding your corpse and planting you without a grave marker or even a minister.

The hole making went slowly and Stout did her share. After a few hours we were barely two feet deep. I'd dug graves in Illinois where the soil was ten feet to clay and a six-foot hole was child's play, but this was real work, and we weren't making much progress in the unyielding hard stony earth.

"We'll have to just cover him up with large rocks," she finally said, wiping the perspiration from her forehead on her gloved hand. "We'll never get the hole deep enough at this rate."

When Badger's remains wrapped in his blankets and ground cloth were finally laid in the grave, I felt some relief. Poor man never owned nothing, never probably had a wife or children of his own. The large part of his life savings was no doubt taken by his killers, and what paltry sum had that been? It wasn't enough to just leave a man's body to the depredation of buzzards and wild animals. The rock piling took a while, too, but we finally felt the job well enough done and stood in exhausted silence at the site.

"Locke." She was pulling on my sleeve. "You're better at words than I am. Say something nice over him since we don't have a preacher or a Good Book on us."

I agreed and we bowed our heads. My words came slowly, and the knot in my throat kept rising up, choking off my speech. I finally managed to say what I hoped would impress Badger's maker that he needed a place in heaven since his death was so senseless.

When I said amen Stout took my right hand and squeezed it. She stood there with tears streaming down her face and shaking her head.

"It ain't fair, Locke, it just ain't fair. Badger was just a bashful cowboy that wanted to herd cows. He never hurt no one."

"They robbed him for what little was on him," I said, holding her fingers in my grip and noticing his horse. "They even turned his saddlebags inside out."

Stout agreed, dabbing at her tears. "Come on, we better get going. We've already lost another half day. They'll be thinking I went south with the supplies."

"Will your family worry about you?"

"Maybe, maybe not. My bunch is busy this week, they've got hay to buck up for our horses' winter feed. They'll figure sooner or later I'll come home wagging my tail behind."

We tied the bay horse on behind. I would have liked to ride him, but since we were conversing so friendly, I didn't want to relinquish my place beside her on the spring seat.

At dark we made a dry camp. Neither of us had said much all afternoon. The murder-robbery had certainly shaken both of us. I whipped out my Colt twice at nothing while we were unhitching and setting up camp.

She looked at me hard the second time I drew the weapon. Her hand gently guided the gun barrel downward. "Those killers have rode on by now, I'm certain."

I agreed.

The weeping evergreen boughs that surrounded us were illuminated by the firelight. We were locked in a world sprayed with stars overhead, the tall shadowy pines like a black fortress around us. Somewhere out where the owls flew were killers—waiting for another victim. Even the fire's heat didn't chase the chill from my body.

"What'll this sheriff do about the murder when he gets the letter?" I asked.

"Not much he can do. He couldn't learn much riding out here either."

"So Badger's death will be just a letter in his files?"

"What would you do? We never saw any signs of who shot him. I guess we could accuse those two sneaking outlaws if they came this way."

I agreed, defeated, but felt very righteous about prosecuting the killers, whoever they were. Some action needed to be taken. I didn't have the slightest idea how it should be done, but I felt obligated to poor dead Badger Jones to do something.

My turn came to stand guard. I pressed my back to the wagon wheel, sat on the ground with the rifle across my lap, and listened to the night sounds. Stout was already asleep in her bedroll. I could hear her easy breathing from under the bed of the wagon. Good. Maybe she'd get some well-deserved rest.

I must have dozed a little. When I awoke with a start, I heard someone sniffing close by. My heart stopped as I listened to a footfall just beyond the edge of our camp. What were they smelling? The fire was nearly out. How long had I napped? Damn. Someone, maybe more than one, was lurking somewhere across the campsite beyond the fire. I studied the star-lighted trees, wondering if there were others sneaking up behind me.

"Stop!" I shouted, imagining the faces of Dingus

and Serval glaring at me across the fire. I leaped to my feet at their throat-clearing sound or whatever I heard. Life or death—the time was at hand. Any moment I expected the cherry red blast of their gun muzzles pointed at me to flash alive in the darkness.

Rapid-firing the Winchester from the waist, I intended to go down fighting as I sprayed the pines with bullets at hip level. I felt the hard recoil against my hip as the long gun spoke death in the night with each levered stroke. I heard someone cry out and hit the ground hard. The hammer finally fell on an empty chamber.

Colt in hand, Stout crawled out from her bedroll to join me.

"My gawd, Locke, what are you shooting at?"

"Someone, something, I told them to stop. I must have got one of them. I heard the bullets hit them." My breath came in ragged gulps; I nearly shook with the tension.

"I'll light the lantern," she said as we both wondered what had fallen in the brush. There were no other sounds as I listened. The palms of my hand were wet with perspiration where I clutched the rifle's stock. Numb with anxiety, I set the empty long gun against the wagon wheel and peered into the night. My knees were weak as I dried my palms on the front of my pants.

I got the Colt ready in my hand while she lighted the lantern. There was no sound from anyone. They must be dead. Well, if they'd have been honorable they'd never have snuck up, sniffing their noses in the night.

"My gawd, you scared the life out of me with that

shooting," Stout said, holding the lamp up. The soft yellow ring of light spread across the ground as she raised the lantern.

"Nothing else I could do but shoot when they didn't answer."

"I know, I'd have done the same thing. Do you see anything?" she asked, holding the light over her head.

"Nope, but I'm certain I hit one of them." I searched around wishing I had eyes in the back of my head in case the other one was behind me, waiting for his chance to get the drop on us. My breath came short and my heart pounded like a trip-hammer as we cautiously moved around the fire.

"I don't doubt you shot someone. Come on, there's bound to be blood if you hit them."

"They never ran off," I assured her as we cautiously edged to the far side of the clearing.

I stopped her. One was laying on his side. I cocked the hammer on the Colt. "There he is."

"Yes," she agreed breathless. Stout raised the lamp higher. The form never moved; it looked very dark. We advanced closer and I saw by the light it was no man.

"Oh, my gawd." Stout started to laugh. "Locke, you've shot a damn black bear."

"Well, he shouldn't have been up here sniffing around our camp," I said, feeling indignant at her assessment and holstering my Colt.

Stout set down the lamp and hugged me. "There ain't nothing wrong with shooting a black bear. It's just I knew you'd killed someone." She looked back at the dead animal and began to laugh again. "Oh, Locke, it's only a black bear."

I held her tight. The opportunity of having her in my arms was worth shooting the damn bear over again. Besides, I began to feel a little heady since I'd never shot a bear before in my life. I'd never even seen one except in circuses before my first game shot in Arizona.

She finally straightened and looked up at me. "You did a good job anyway."

"What'll we do with him?"

"Butcher him and pack him out. We'll find someone needs some meat and they can have him."

"Are they good to eat?" I asked, trying to remember Jerome's teaching on bear meat.

"Not bad. I'll cook some for breakfast. Let's go get the skinning knife and tools from the wagon."

The copper smell of blood and guts clung to my hands and became embedded in my nose. My muscles were sore from the skinning and the cutting. The sun caught us with the bear's carcass quartered and stowed in the back of the wagon under the tarp to keep cool as possible. The black furry hide was piled on top of the canvas cover to dry.

"That bear's skin would make a good coat to wear in the winter," Stout said. Bear meat sizzled in her skillet. I sat on the ground and tried to remember how I had ever imagined a bear had been a human sneaking into our camp. Guess I'd get more experienced.

"That smell ever leave the fur?" I asked, wrinkling my nose and wondering if one would stink like a bear when wearing it?

"Wouldn't smell at all except when it gets wet or in a warm room." She laughed.

"You can have it," I said, and yawned. We still faced another long day's drive. "How far will we get today?"

"I hope Strawberry Creek."

"What's at Strawberry Creek?"

"Oh, it's a nice stream. We can rest the horses there for a half day then push on since we'll still be a day and half from home."

"How do you ever find your cattle in this country? That is your business, cattle not sheep?"

"Sheep? Whoever mentioned sheep?" She looked aghast at me.

"Jed in Babbett's store asked me if I was going to sheep or cattle ranch."

"Well, if you're going to raise sheep, you just get your old stinking bear guts out of my wagon! I ain't hauling no damn woolly gopher-chasing rascal with me. Why didn't you say that you were going into the sheep business to start with? I'd sure left your stinking hide behind in Flagstaff."

I stood up, stepped to her, and hugged her in a bear hug. I was so furious I fumed. "I ain't no stinking sheep man, never have been. I come here to be a rancher—listen—listen to me—" Then I kissed her hard on the mouth.

She hit me on the ear with that turner in her hand and it stung. It was all worth it as I hugged the breath out of her. She knocked my hat off trying to stop me, but I didn't quit kissing her. Not until I had enough for the time being. Then I finally let her loose.

She held the back of her hand to her mouth as if I'd

burned her lips and looked at me bewildered. I never saw her look like that before. I meant to kiss her, it wasn't a whimsical thing. I'd have done it at Mormon Lake, but I didn't have all my nerve up then like I did after working shoulder to shoulder with her butchering that dang bear.

"You figure you can just kiss me whenever you want! Well I'll tell you something right now, Locke McTavish—you can't!" and she stomped out of camp.

I had to get my jackknife out because she still had the turner in her hand when she went away, and the bear meat needed to be turned over. She would come to her senses and return. It was, however, small solace to eat that greasy pork-tasting bear a piece at a time while she sulked off in the woods and I was left to myself in camp.

I finally got my back up and went to look for Miss Rice. If she thought I was out to ruin her reputation or take advantage of her, I wanted that impression corrected. When I rounded the wagon I saw Stout was returning to camp; I could see the hard set to her jaw. We met about the wagon tongue and circled each other with our heads kinda stuck out like fighting geese. We straddled across the tongue chasing each other in a circle.

"You can take Badger's horse and just ride on your merry way." She pointed for me to leave.

"I am not going to grow sheep."

"I don't care. I ain't going to be around you." She sidestepped over the wagon tongue and I kept after her. "Locke McTavish, you can raise all the sheep you want to raise, where ever you want, except not in North Cut or around me!"

"Listen!" I pointed my index finger at her as we warily circled around. "I'm not some sheep farmer, I'm a cattleman, and I come to Arizona to do that, and if I want to raise cattle right there in North Cut next door to you, how are you going to stop me?"

"By damn I'll stop you, you lecherous devil. Kissing me like . . ."

"Like what?"

"Like you were *somebody!*" She made a swing in the air with her fist as if she'd struck me with her balled-up hand.

"Well, I don't hide my feelings."

"Feelings? You don't have any feeling. I'm not some doxy from the—the whorehouse you can just grab up and handle."

"I didn't do that!"

"Well." She was pointing her finger at me as we moved around a little faster. "You certainly treated me like I was one!"

"I did not! I kissed you!"

"Who asked you to?" Her blue eyes were nearly flooded.

"I wanted to—"

She stopped and dropped her head, looking suspiciously at me. "Why?"

"Because I have high intentions for us."

"Us?" she asked, crestfallen, and stood with her chin down.

"Dammit, Stout Rice, I'm courting you."

"I never asked—"

I made the move to be beside her. "Can we harness the horses and go on?" I asked, hugging her shoulder.

"I guess so," she said, slipping out from under my arm. "But I'm warning you, Locke McTavish, I'll not be taken lightly."

I nodded in agreement. She would not be taken lightly nor with force either.

CHAPTER

5

Huge rock formations rose above the single track road like storybook illustrations of great European castles from the books I had read in my youth. As we went along, I silently gave the giant forms names like Strom's Castle and McBryde's Own Fort. There were so many that no mapmaker could have christened all of them with names. I never imagined so much unused space existed.

Stout pointed out a mule deer that bounded up a hillside, his great rack barely out of the velvet. The animal's wide antlers resembled the red deer of England I'd seen in circuses. Truly, the frontier held many more treasures than one ever saw in Illinois or the middle states of this country.

"In fall and winter, when the weather cools and the meat keeps, we always have a deer hanging on our back porch for meat," she said. "They're good eating."

"I've had venison before. Where are we camping tonight?"

"Strawberry Creek, McFee's bottoms. There's some trout in it. If you're any good at fishing, we might have some for supper," she said, handing me the reins to drive for a while.

"Do you have hooks?" I asked, wondering why she hadn't mentioned the fact she had such stock at Mormon Lake.

"A few, and some catgut line you can use."

"Fishing would be my forte, as they say in France." I could dream all day about trout. I'd heard my grandfather speak of his trout-fishing days in Scotland with my father, who was a boy at the time.

"I suppose you've been to France too?" she asked.

"No, I've never been there, but I'd love to go see the art treasures in the Louvre."

She glanced over at me and then shook her head. "That's where you and I differ. I've been to Flagstaff. That's the biggest town I've ever been in, and I'm so damn glad to get back to North Cut, you couldn't hire me to leave there."

"This North Cut must be some place."

"It is. You'll see if we ever get there."

"I'm slowing you down getting home, aren't I?"

She shook her head and turned to check our back trail. Then she settled back down. "No, I've been glad you came along—most of the time," she qualified her appreciation. "I've made this trip three times by myself and never had a problem. Oh, one of my sisters, either Erv or Tate, usually comes along, but we never have a thing happen. You and I have been plagued with trouble since, well, since I met you."

"I didn't plan it that way."

Stout nodded in approval. "I know."

"How much do ranches cost?"

"You got a big bankroll?" she asked, acting relaxed and her own self again.

"No."

"Then you'll have to start small and build up. Get yourself a few mother cows and a bull first. You start to save she-stock, then in ten years, if they don't die in a drought or snowstorm and no one steals them, you should have a couple hundred mother cows."

"How do you buy this land?"

"You don't. You homestead a place, build a cabin, make repairs each year, and in five years you'll own it. I don't know of a place for sale in the North Cut."

"Just stake out the land?"

"Sure, I'll help you do that if you don't plan to run sheep."

I scowled at her. "I am not going to grow any sheep!"

She looked over at me wistfully and pursed her lips together. "Ain't they got lots of sheep in Scotland?"

"They've got cattle there too, and besides, I've never been to Scotland. I was born in Illinois and lived there all my life."

"Could have fooled me. At times I swear you sound just like Barney McFee."

"Who's he?"

"A Scotsman who lives on North Cut."

"He raise sheep?"

"No, he makes whiskey."

"Ah, another skill of my ancestors." I looked over at her and smiled, grateful her anger was gone again.

"You'll meet him soon enough. We'll lay over in his meadows this afternoon. One thing, if you're so all-fired certain you want to be a rancher, you'll need to send for a brand."

"To mark the cattle's hide with?" I asked, holding back the team on down the grade and working the brake to ease their load.

"That's it. You get that iron red hot and burn the hair back till the scar reads like good saddle leather on their hide, and you have them marked for life."

"How do you restrain them?" I asked as we crossed a dry creek bed and started up the grade.

"Restrain them?" She looked at me as if I'd again lost my good senses.

"Hold them down."

"Oh, you rope them. You'll have to learn to throw a lariat too."

"Is it hard to do?"

"Kinda like walking—you probably fell down several times learning how to do that."

"Very good," I said. I felt I was accomplishing something on this portion of the trip toward my future as a stockman in this land.

"You've got a helluva lot to learn in a short time," she said, and waited for my answer.

"I'm a fast learner," I said flippantly. We both laughed as the wagon tossed us from side to side while wallowing over the ruts and boulders in the roadway. There was a sizable mountain ahead, and the road looked like it clung to the bare face of the sheer cliffs. It was a sobering thing to observe, especially to a man from the flatlands. Dread soured my stomach as I considered the way ahead, but I was bound not to let her know of my concern.

We paused several times on the long pulls and rested the horses on the steep grade climbing the mountain's face. The sheer side of the mountain on our right towered to dazzling heights. On the left the same yellow tan rock wall dropped steeply away until the valley below looked ever more distant each step of the way.

"What if you meet someone?" I asked, wondering how two vehicles could ever pass without one going off the edge.

She shook her head. "Hell, Locke, why think of all the damn bad things. We'll be to the top in another hour."

"Yes, ma'am." The knot in my throat wasn't eased any by her lack of an answer to my question. What would we do?

I spoke to the team and the horses eased into their collars as if they, too, respected our position on the very narrow thread of road, certain death being the answer for any misstep or foolishness. Stout must have trusted me with the lines because she let me drive. Still, my knees were nearly quaking and my stomach sour as we gained more altitude. I guessed being on high places was part of being in the West. I'd have to acclimate myself to the fact.

When the iron-rimmed wagon wheel rolled over a rock and dropped the wagon down with a jar on the other side, an action you just accepted on a nice level road, I drew a deep breath and thanked God for not rocking me out of the seat. The spring seat we rode on normally absorbed the worst of the bumps and tossed us together by the motion. That jolting around usually was nice seated closely beside Stout. However, on the road up Strawberry Hill, those lurches by the wagon made me wonder if we would be pitched out into space and fall to our sure death.

The steady team lumbered up the sharp grade. The narrow ledge we drove on circled around the mountain to the right so we could not see what was ahead. I knew I'd never make a good eagle or buzzard because we were about as high up as they flew, and I didn't like it one bit.

My heart ran too fast and my breath could hardly keep up. I must have moved to the front portion of the seat a dozen times wanting to help the big horses pull the load. Antsy was what my mother would have called my actions when I was a boy.

"Locke, sit back and relax, for heaven's sake." My mother would have admonished me like that. However, my mother had never been in the Arizona mountains either. I figured she'd have wrung a white handkerchief to death going up this damn hill.

"There's the top." Stout pointed to a broad spot in the timbered vee ahead of us. "We can rest up there."

I rose up for one last view of the country behind us, a majestic land of mountain ranges, some dark with forest, others blood red barren buttes. Badger's horse was trailing along like he was on the flats, nothing bothered him. About the time I stood up to see more of the bottom of the canyon, the off front wheel rolled over a rock. The action tossed me to the right, and I landed squarely in Stout's lap on the drop.

"See any boogers back there?" Stout grinned as she righted me.

"No," I said, a little red-faced, hurriedly rising to straighten my reins and get reseated.

"I'm always glad to get that part of the road behind me," she said.

I glanced over at her. Stout was looking straight ahead and grasping her knees in her hands. She hadn't liked that treacherous stretch any more than I had, probably why she had me drive. I knew that on the flat ahead, when we stopped to blow the team, I would make a trail for some privacy. My innards were needing some relief.

Midafternoon, collie dogs with long slender noses —like they had in the Scottish Highlands—came barking at us as we drove up the lane to the McFee place. The splashes of white and brown on the dogs' coats looked as if they'd been made by a painter. Ah, sleek-coated, well-fed animals—I enjoyed the sight of them. A scattering of log buildings and pens under some tall pines made up the ranch. The cackle of hens about the place were the familiar sounds that reminded me of home for a moment.

"Stout, me girl!" a red-faced man shouted, coming across the yard. He reminded me of a man I knew in Illinois. Stout jumped down and shook his hand like a boy would.

"I want you to meet a friend of mine, Barney," she said. "Locke McTavish—he plans to start ranching in this country."

"I say, laddie, you have a good name there." I thanked him and we shook hands, though I still had the reins in one hand and sat on the seat. Stout had said we'd go on down in the bottoms to camp for the night. I was anxious to test my skills on the fish in these waters.

While Stout talked of pleasantries with the man, I noticed a short shapely girl of maybe fifteen come out on the porch. She had fiery red hair and a splash of freckles, and she looked curiously in my direction. She waved at Stout and they exchanged words.

"McFee says he can use your bear meat," Stout said to me. "Is that all right?"

"Fine," I said, not certain I wanted more of the fatty substance. "You can have all of it."

"We like it made into sausage," McFee said as I tied off the reins and jumped down to help them unload the meat.

"Might be good that way," I agreed.

I carried a hind quarter to the cellar behind the man, his arms also full of bear meat.

"Locke, this is McFee's daughter, Kathreen," Stout said as the redhead joined us to help.

"You're new here?" she asked as if anxious to make conversation.

"Yes, ma'am. I arrived in Flagstaff a few days ago."

"How did you meet Stout?" she asked, quickly catching my stride to walk beside me.

"Kathreen, the man's business is his own," her father scolded.

"It's all right," I said to save her. "We met in Flagstaff. One man was beating another. Actually kicking another. Anyway, I broke it up."

Kathreen looked up at me with her green eyes like she was very impressed.

"They were outlaws, it turns out," Stout said quickly as we waited for McFee to come out of the cellar and take the strong-smelling meat we held for him.

"Outlaws?" McFee asked as he raised up, exiting the cellar's low doorway.

"Yes, Marshal Floyd Tillman came by and told us they were killers and robbers," Stout said.

"And you fought with them?" Kathreen swooned.

"Well, I had a short round with one of them and luckily I won," I said, feeling in a peculiarly tight situation with Kathreen acting so impressed with my actions.

"Don't let him kid you," Stout said to her. "Locke is a fist-throwing dude."

"They were killers and you stood up to them with your bare fists. My, my," Kathreen said.

"Here," I said, handing the heavy quarter to McFee when he reappeared. I was free to get out of this clutch and wanted to leave rather quickly.

"Oh, Barney, someone robbed and killed Badger Jones on the road," Stout said. "We found him yesterday and buried him."

"Not Badger!" Kathreen said, looking wide-eyed and shocked.

Stout nodded. "They backshot him."

McFee came out of the cellar shaking his head. "That was a good boy. He came by here not two days ago on his way to Flagstaff, I guess. Mighty shame that this country is overrun with riffraff and criminals who'd do wicked things like that."

With the bear meat secure in McFee's storage, we thanked them and got ready to be on our way across the pastureland and to the bottoms. If I'd been interested in Kathreen, I was sure I could have struck more words with her. But the only woman on my mind was the cowgirl who climbed up to share the wagon seat with me. We waved good-bye and drove out of the yard, the friendly collies barking at our heels.

"She likes you," Stout said, looking dead ahead.

"You mean Kathreen?"

"Who else could I mean?"

"Not interested," I said, and drew a deep breath through my nose.

"If you're going to ranch up here, you should look around. There's several eligible girls up here."

"She's a mere child. How old? Fifteen or maybe fourteen even?"

"Lots of men—"

"Is that the stream down there?" I asked sharply as I observed the cottonwoods and the sycamores that lined the far end of the bottom.

"You don't want to talk about it?"

"You said there were fish there."

"You don't have to get your back up. Yes, there are fish in the creek, and they're damn hard to catch."

I glanced over at her. Her arms were all folded and she was in a big huff—I'd show her fishing.

CHAPTER
6

The small stream rushed over and around large rocks, even poured over dropoffs like waterfalls. Grandfather had described Scottish streams like this one. I stood back a little awed, for the creek was very narrow compared to Illinois fishing places. The elusive trout were in fast, cold water. My heart pounded as I considered my plan of actions.

Feed would be the first consideration—what did they eat? Then I saw a hapless brown grasshopper flounder into the water rather than land on the rock he intended. There was a swirl of swift silver, and a fat trout had him for his dinner. The answer settled, I hurried back to the wagon for Stout's offer of hooks and line. My mind set, I knew how I'd capture some trout.

"The fish in this creek are hard to catch," she announced, handing me the small steel hooks and the roll of fine line from her war bag.

"Oh, yes," I agreed.

"Should I grease the skillet or not?" she asked, looking me in the eye.

"We'll have to see. I've never fished for them before."

"I'll bet you don't catch a—"

"I'll bet all one night's dances at that schoolhouse, then you're on," I said, and with the fishing gear in my hand, left her looking perplexed.

"Hey, you owe me several of those dances now!" she shouted after my back.

I did? Well that was nice news. There were times I thought I was winning Stout over to my way of thinking and times when I could swear I hadn't made an inch of ground with that woman.

A sturdy but flexible willow stick was needed for a pole. I found a suitable one, stripped bark, limbs, and leaves away with my jackknife. I tied on line and hook while listening to the rush of the brook over the rocks like a symphony orchestra playing. This was rather heady business—to be on the frontier and to apply my skills to trout fishing.

The damn grasshoppers were everywhere until you wanted one. They popped up, soared in head-high hops when I tried to capture them, then they were gone. Using my hat for a trap and running about a considerable amount, I managed to finally capture three. Two crawly ones I stored in my vest pocket, the third I impaled on the hook.

I took off my gun belt, boots, and socks, rolled my pants up to my knees, and began to sneak up on the water with my stark white, barkless pole in hand. With the tempting hopper on the hook and some twelve feet of line on the end of a six-foot rod, I was ready to catch fish.

The water was cold on my feet as I eased in the stream. Fish upstream was the first rule. Fish are lazy, my paw had told me. They would be behind a rock out of the current waiting for the water to bring them their supper.

I swung the hefty grasshopper over my head and let him touch the water to begin his wild ride down the swirls and rills of the flow. I held my breath standing oh so still. As he floated by the large partially submerged rock, lightning struck, and a hungry denizen rose to the occasion with a splash of water. The rod dipped with the strike.

I felt the muscular tug as the steel barb speared his mouth and he fought the restraint in shock. He flipped twice out of the water in a shower of spray that shone in rainbow-colored droplets. The trout's downstream direction forced me to turn around cautiously on the slick, mossy bottom. Finally, I hefted him up and out on the bank, his silver gill covers open wide gasping for air. My first trout! It was less than a pound, but all the heart-stirring feeling my father had promised me was right there in Strawberry Creek.

I admired the fish for a long while before I made a stringer from a willow branch and let him stay in the water while I went for the second one.

Careful not to disturb the other fish, I eased back in the stream to see if more of my trout's relatives were at the same rock. But it was to no avail, so I waded upstream, trying other sites. The cold water numbed my toes and shins, but I made no complaints as I lost the other two hoppers to quick-thinking trout. One caught to three escapees was the score, and the trout were winning as I waded out and went to capture more bait.

Standing on the bank, the choice was mine. I could plunder around after grasshoppers in the stiff grass and burrs barefooted or go pull on my boots. Since I only needed a few insects for bait, I decided to do it barefooted. With my pole set aside and my hat ready to net them, I stalked the elusive hopper. Winching at the barbs and jabs to my soles, I finally half ran on my tiptoes to avoid exposure to the sharp projectiles as I hurried after the damn hopper.

"Well, my gawd, is that a dance?" Stout asked, coming down the high bank.

I frowned at her. "Get down here and help me catch some of these grasshoppers if you want fish for supper."

"You mean you caught one already?"

I stopped. "Easy as you shoot rabbits. Help me capture a few hoppers and I'll show you how to fish."

Stout could catch a grasshopper on the wing with her bare hands and soon had a half dozen gathered for me. I made tender steps back to the tethered trout and showed her.

"He's real nice," she said, impressed.

"Take off your boots up here, and I'll give you a lesson in fishing. I've spooked the fish in this hole, but there's others."

"I can't believe you catch them on grasshoppers," she said.

"They eat them."

"Oh, I guess so, but we always used red meat."

I frowned and stored the information. We stopped at my pole, and I pointed where we would enter the water and how we'd fish above a large rock. I waited for a second because she wasn't taking off her boots.

"Well, turn your head," she said, "I'm shedding these britches, too, so I can wade in there with you."

"Yes, ma'am," I said, turning my back to her. Her hand rested on my back for balance as she removed her boots and pants from under her skirt. I felt honored to be chosen, but there wasn't a tree close either.

"You go first," I directed in a whisper. "Be very careful. The creek bottom is certainly slick."

I noticed she shared my tender soles, and we crept to the water's edge on pained steps. She gathered her skirt up between her legs and went knee-deep in the water with me right behind her. I lifted the pole to swing the baited hook upstream.

"Like this," I said, and dropped the insect in place so he would be taken downstream and around the swirl that rounded the large rock. "Here," I let her hold the pole. "Watch for him. He'll be quick."

I put my hand over hers to set the hook as I watched the hopper's downstream course from over her shoulder. The hopper swam and was swept by the current until he was right above the large rock. I raised her rod tip a little as the muscles in my neck tightened in expectation.

The explosion broke like a gunshot. The largest trout I could imagine boiled up, took the bait, and the hook held. The willow pole bent double, and Stout screamed aloud, "Oh hell, it's a whale, Locke!"

"Yes, follow him! Go or he'll break the line or the pole!" I screamed.

Stout turned with both her hands gripping the wobbling stick as the trout broke water and lunged in the air. The silver reflection looked like it came off a large mirror in the sun. Stout headed into the deeper water that fast was up to her waist. Her skirt floated up around her. The wiggling pole bent in a U, yet she looked as determined as anyone I'd ever seen, holding her rod tight.

"Damn you!" she swore as the big fish changed direction and she was forced to turn. I was in the water beside her, stumbling on the mossy bottom to keep out of her way as the veteran trout sought all ways to get loose.

"Keep your rod up!" I shouted and pointed at him.

Then I saw the line snap in a fine mist that sprayed both of us as the pole whipped up. We were both standing on our toes in the stream, water to our armpits. We looked at each other and the emptiness set in—we'd lost him.

Disappointment struck. Stout shook her head, then I saw the shocked look on her face. She'd lost her footing and slipped under the water. Stout bobbed up, blowing water out of her mouth. I took the pole and smiled at her.

"You did that on purpose!"

Despite my denial, there was something mean in the set of her eyes, and I knew nothing would satisfy her but dunking me. My move backwards was a mistake; my feet went out, and the cold water engulfed me. I settled to my butt on the bottom. Clear water that the sun shone through was all above me. You could see everything including her face looking down at me. Strawberry Creek was certainly unlike the rivers in Illinois that were silty all the time.

I floundered up and took a quick breath. Stout was swimming to shallow water. I waded out with the pole still in my hand. Her soaked clothes clung to her as she pushed her wet hair back from her face.

"Locke McTavish, other than near drowning me, you are a right good trout fisherman."

"Thank you. Shall I clean the first one and let it cook while we dry out?"

"I wish I'd got the big one," she said, shaking her head and holding her dark skirt out. "You'll have to tell them at home how big he was. They'll probably think I'm lying. Yes, bring it along. I have beans cooking. I never before saw anyone quite that good at fishing." Stout looked at me, impressed, before she turned and went to camp.

"Next time," I promised her and went pained in small testy steps for my boots and gun. Enough of this barefoot business for me. "We'll catch him."

The trout proved wonderful. I savored every bite of the flaky, firm meat. We shared him on a plate between us as we sat cross-legged and faced each other in the last hours of daylight. Red shafts of light off the mountains above us lanced into the bottoms like fire spears.

A whippoorwill called in the growing darkness. I listened and thought of the family farm at home— nothing like this wild land. There were no trout in those rivers, just bass, small perch, and whiskered catfish, but no trout. In some places in Europe, or so I'd heard, only kings were allowed to fish for them.

"What happened to McFee's wife?" I asked, recalling we had not seen one, only the girl. "I mean, does he have one?"

"She ran away with the tin man."

"The who?"

"You know, the tin man that comes around with a peddler wagon and solders up the holes in your cooking pots and pans. Oh, he sells thread, has some calico material, and sharpens knives and scissors too."

"Yes, we have them in Illinois. But she left with one of them? Was he handsome or what?"

Stout shrugged when I questioned her with my eyes. "Guess she was just tired of being in one place too long. Folks are like that, you know?"

"Didn't McFee go after her?"

"He told my father," Stout said, then gave a big deep exhale, "Margaret wasn't ever happy in this country, and if she was happy with the tin man, then God bless her."

"Did you know her?"

"Yes."

"How long ago did she go?"

"Maybe five years or so."

"Why didn't the girl go along?"

Stout didn't look at me; she acted busy feeding herself. Finally, she looked up and swept the hair back from her face. "Her mother said Kathreen was too much like her father and didn't want to have to look at her the rest of her life and be reminded of him."

I didn't ask anymore. The fish didn't taste quite as good as before. We were only a day and a half from the end of our odyssey, and I wasn't wanting it to end. I'd have to think of something.

CHAPTER

7

Dawn was still concealed by the mountains to the east when we pulled out through the McFees' homestead. They waved. Kathreen bore a milk pail on her arm as she came from the cabin. She flagged us a good-bye. No doubt Kathreen was headed for the jersey cow I noticed in a small pasture nearby. The collies all barked as the iron-rimmed wheels rolled along headed for the Rice ranch. We were a day and a half away from their place, according to my guide and mentor, Stout.

"Who does he sell whiskey to?" I asked as we pulled on the road.

"Anyone that has the money, I guess. I'm surprised he didn't offer you some in trade for that bear meat." Stout had that look-ahead stare in her eyes when she talked. Something was eating her up inside whenever she did that.

"Am I treading on sacred grounds?"

"No, I guess not. I like Barney and always felt sorry his wife left him, but I've had some harsh words with him in the past two years."

I waited for her to continue, this wasn't easy for her to tell me, and I wanted to hear all of it. There was something I was going to learn, something deeper than the frivolous things I'd heard up until then.

"See, my father is bad to drink at times—well, he gets all bound up, and then he gets to talking about my mother dying and leaving him all alone."

"You said that she died years ago?"

"Don't matter. He still gets drunk over her memory, or at least that's his excuse."

I knew of such men. "And Barney sells him the whiskey?"

"Exactly. Last roundup, Pa got so drunk he fell off his horse and was laid up for a week. He could have been seriously hurt."

"I see." I understood about folks and their problems—we all had them.

"You know, Locke, I'd never have brought you along if I figured you drank like that."

I glanced at her as the wagon lumped over a bump and gave us a good pitch together. "How did you know that I didn't have a thirst?"

"Because after the fight you went and bought clothes instead of going for a drink." Stout started laughing. "Most men would have finished that fight and needed a drink. I even thought when you named it—ah, haberdasher—that it was some kinda saloon."

We both laughed as the wagon road wound through the pine-forested valley and started up the next grade. I wondered if she knew that very first time I saw her, Stout's beauty made me even forget there was such a thing as liquor. Someday I'd tell her and convince her of my intentions. I clucked for the horses to jog.

Stout promised I'd be looking down on the North Cut basin by late afternoon.

Ever been to the edge of the world? In midafternoon as she had promised me, we came to where Arizona tilted up in an enormous escarpment. From the edge of the world I looked across a million acres, Stout called this endless line the Mongollon Rim—*Muggy-own* was how she said it. I felt awed viewing so much forested land and blue-black mountains in a profusion beneath us.

"Welcome to North Cut," she said proudly.

"It's quite a place. I see why you hate to leave it."

"We needed some wire to build a new corral, a little horse feed for the fall roundup and some staples, but you've seen the things I brought. There's a store down the basin where we buy most of our needs."

"No town?"

"No, but the Mormons will probably build one someday."

"Mormons? I thought they were all in Utah?"

"No, they're all over. Several families of them settled on the North Cut. They homesteaded places so they could farm and irrigate. They're farmers, for the most part."

Since a boy, I'd heard lots of stories about the Mormons. There had been bloodshed and bitterness years before in Illinois between them and the other Christian people. Folks at home mentioned Mormons like a cross between the plague and heathen hordes. I wondered what they looked like.

"We'll be at Charlie Brackett's before dark," she said, slapping the big horses with the lines.

"He another rancher?" I asked.

"Oh, yes, he's a bachelor, and every time we go there my sisters and I end up doing ten weeks' worth of dirty dishes to have something to eat out of." She shook her head ruefully. "He has this skinny old cowboy, Sonny Pitts, who works for him. I hate for Sonny to even come to those dances. See, Sonny don't ever try to dance till he's in the chips, and then he can't even scoot his boots around, he has to lift them up knee-high."

"Nice guys?"

"Oh, they're the salt of the earth—" She acted like she wanted to say something more, then she shook her head.

"What's wrong?"

"Why does there have to be something wrong?" she asked.

"The way you clammed up."

"I'm still talking."

"No you started to say something. What was it?"

She looked at me in a scowl. "Well, bringing you along ain't the smartest thing I've ever done."

"You want me to ride in on Badger's horse."

"No! That Kathreen McFee won't let her dress hit her rump till she tells everyone from hell to breakfast I drug this new dude up here."

"Looks bad, I mean for your reputation?"

"I don't give a damn about my reputation. I am who I am! And I do what I want to do! It's the gawdamn teasing those cowboys like Charlie Brackett will bring down on me for dragging you along."

"I can straighten them out."

She waved my defense aside with her gloved hand. "No, it ain't the fighting kinda teasing. It's just outright getting under your skin for a laugh is all they do it for. Hell, it wouldn't hurt a bit, but I ain't got nothing on them is all."

Stout shook her head and flicked the horses to hurry a little. The ring of the harness metal, the creak of the leather, and hum of the wheels accompanied us. We were headed for Charlie Brackett's place, dirty dishes and all, I guessed.

When I looked to check our backtrail, I realized how proud I was to be on the seat with her. Badger's old horse was still bringing up the rear, and there was no sign of Dingus or Seawell. Maybe they wouldn't come to the North Cut. The closer we got to this place, the less concerned Stout showed about them being around, like this was a haven. I sure hoped so.

My first impression of Charlie Brackett's ranch was that it looked like a fallen-down junkyard. Elk and deer antlers were nailed all over the house. The sod roof sagged badly in the center like a deep valley. The porch had been repeatedly propped up with crooked poles. A couple of black stock dogs ran out to threaten us with their barks. A man in his forties wearing his flannel underwear and britches with the galluses down came out on the porch. She didn't tell me as he stood

Dusty Richards

picking his teeth but I guessed I'd just seen Charlie
Brackett for the first time.

"Hey, Stout!" Charlie waved to her and spit off in
our direction when we stopped. "You never said you
was going after a mail-order groom. Sonny, get the
hell out here! You'll never believe what Stout Rice
found in Flagstaff! Lord have mercy, Stout's got her a
fellar."

Stout gave me a cold look and shook her head over
our private secret. Vengeance in her eyes, she climbed
down off that wagon. Then she stalked to the house
with her finger pointed like a gun at the laughing
rancher.

"You and that dried-up old prune of a cowboy say
one more word you'll not get one sourdough biscuit!
Not one, Charlie!"

The rancher wiped at the tears coming down his
face hardly able to recover. "Who the hell is he?"

"Let him tell you," Stout said, and swept by him
through the front door into the house.

"Locke McTavish, sir," I said, climbing down and
holding out my hand.

Charlie put up his galluses before he lost his pants
and shook my hand. "Nice to meet you. You ride all
the way from the railhead with that ornery woman?"

"Yes sir."

"Damn, boy, you're a glutton for punishment. She's
in there right now tearing up my nice kitchen. Hear
her? Chewing out poor Sonny for being a little behind
doing the dishes."

The main room looked like a bachelor place when I
stepped inside. There was an unmade bed in the

72

middle of the room, a dusty giant bear head mounted over the fireplace. The hearth opening was streaked with soot because the chimney didn't draw properly or perhaps because sometimes the fire got too large.

A bowlegged cowboy thin as a fence slat came past me with a curt nod, mumbling to himself about how bad womenfolks were around a place, and headed for the front door. I noticed he wore a new-looking shirt that was buttoned to his thin skinny throat.

"McTavish!" she shouted, noisily stoking the stove. "Your hands ain't broke. Come help me."

I looked at Brackett and grinned. He nodded like he had other business. I went to help the lady. When I rounded the half wall, I saw what she meant. There were stacks of dirty dishes everywhere, piled up precariously in random places; pots were all about with utensils poking out of them. There couldn't have been a single clean one left. The crude shelves around the kitchen were bare.

Stout slammed down the lid on the iron stove. "I told you so!"

"Yes, ma'am," I said, afraid to say anything else in the face of her anger. A drop of water on Stout Rice's head would have sizzled.

She rolled up her sleeves to her elbows, then plunged them in the soapy water and scoured each individual plate and pan. I did my part drying while she worked with a fury. Between the tin ones and glazed pottery, Brackett must have had ten sets of dishes. I placed them on the shelves. It amazed me how fast we consumed the mess. Pots and utensils hung from hooks overhead on the open rafters.

The table was finally cleared and scoured by Stout and the dishes were all put up. I looked forward to eating the sweet-smelling sourdough bread in the oven and the cured ham Charlie brought out of his cellar for her to cook. Brackett watched himself around her though, like he expected her to jab him with a sharp fork as punishment for his transgressions. I was damn glad when the dishwashing and drying was over.

We all sat at the table for the meal. Sonny wore a sheet for a bib to keep his new shirt clean. It was tied around his neck and looked like a barber cloth. Brackett kept watching Stout go back and forth after she ordered all of us to sit down and she began to serve the food.

"Tell him the bad news about Badger," she said after setting the pan with the steaming ham in front of Charlie. "You can slice it, can't you?" she asked him.

"Oh yes, ma'am, I can. What about Badger?"

"Someone shot him in the back on the road coming here. Guess he was going to the railhead, huh?"

"Drygulched Badger Jones?" Sonny asked in his nasal voice. "Why, who'd ever do such a thing as that?"

"Mormons," Brackett said, busy carving the red stringy ham away from the white bone.

"No, robbers did it, we figure," I said, curious why he said Mormons.

"Who?" Sonny asked, putting a bony hand covered with liver spots on my sleeve. "That boy Badger didn't have one enemy in this whole country. I knew him well. But I don't believe the Mormons did it. He never hurt them none."

"They did it!" Brackett said, and shook his head. "Those sod-busting, snobbish damn Mormons are behind half the trouble we have in this basin."

Stout shook her head for me in disapproval of Brackett's accusations when she brought the bread.

"That ain't so, Charlie. You thought they were the rustlers last year and it wasn't them at all, remember?" She placed the fresh sliced bread on the table. Impatient with him for not answering her, Stout slapped his hand when the rancher reached for her bread. "Isn't that right?"

"You can coddle them if you want to, girl, but we never had a problem until they moved in here. I'd rather have Geronimo back as have those sneaky bastards around."

"I don't think Geronimo was ever here," she said, folding her skirt under her to sit down, still looking displeased at Brackett. "You old men get things all mixed up. The Chiricahua Apaches weren't ever in these mountains."

"Listen, girl, you aren't that old. Your dad, mother, and I came to this country there were plenty of those black painted-faced savages ready to put an arrow in our asses."

"There was then," Sonny agreed. "I can tell you I got an arrow still stuck in my back from one of them. Never killed me, though. Dang, it hurts sometimes. They couldn't get it out."

"The doctor?" I asked the old man.

"Oh no. Lord, there wasn't any doctor except in Flagstaff. Two cowboys dug with their jackknives in my back for a couple of hours. That sure hurt and they run out of whiskey so we forgot about it." Sonny reached back to feel something. He bolted up straight like someone poked him. "Yeah, it's still in there. I felt it just then."

"Well, why haven't you had it cared for? I mean, had a doctor take it out when you went to Flagstaff."

Sonny ducked his head and looked in Stout's direction, then lowered his voice. "Got busy and forgot about it when I got there." He nodded his head like that was the best answer he had for me and went to forking ham in his mouth.

"Are there any Apaches still around?" I asked.

"No, they shipped the bad ones to Florida a year ago," Charlie said.

"Geronimo and his band? I saw pictures of him in the newspaper." I looked at the two men, amazed that Apaches had shot Sonny. Lord knew about Brackett's adventures.

"You don't reckon the government will ship the damn Mormons to the same prison?" Brackett asked.

"Don't listen to him, Locke. The man is a troublemaker!" Stout shook her head in disapproval. "The Mormons aren't hurting any of us in this basin."

Brackett waved his fork at her. "You defend them if you want to, sister, but they're a plague on this earth. You wait and see! Mark my words, McTavish, they've lulled the likes of her into believing they're pious, holy, religious people, but they ain't!"

"Can we eat in peace?" Stout demanded. "We've had enough trouble the past four days. Outlaws harassed us at Mormon Lake. Locke had to shoot a damn black bear in our camp the other night. Badger Jones dead. I'm not in a mood to argue about Mormons."

"A bear in camp?" Sonny asked, busy eating. "Lucky there ain't many grizzlies left."

"They're fierce animals, I hear. You ever seen one?" I asked.

Sonny looked up and blinked his weak eyes. "I never stayed around much to see them. But one clawed my horse's rump up bad, with him and I running full out to get away from him. Them grizzlies ain't ever nice acting."

"That's a grizzly in there on the fireplace," Brackett said between bites. "Stood up eight foot tall, and I had to shoot him seven times. He kept coming."

"Bet you was getting worried then, huh, boss?" Sonny asked.

"Yes, all I had left was the empty Winchester, and I was going to feed him that gun next. He was close enough to eat it when he finally fell on his face not six feet in front of me."

I could only imagine a wounded eight-foot-tall bear still coming at Brackett. The notion nothing would stop the grizzly must have been awfully sickening.

"We need to get an early start in the morning," Stout said, rising from her chair with a scraping sound. "We won't be disturbing you. I'm already a day late getting back, and it'll be late when we get there anyway. One of those flour barrels on the wagon are yours along with two sacks of brown beans."

"We'll set them off. But Stout, we were just getting to know Mr. McTavish here," Brackett said, wiping his mouth on his sleeve and standing up. "You going to light around here, I guess?"

"He means are you staying in the basin," Stout said to explain.

"I plan to take up ranching," I said.

"Oh yeah, oh yeah," Brackett said, looking like something was wrong or his stomach was upset.

"You all right?" I asked, concerned.

"Sure. Fine. Let's get those goods off the wagon, huh?"

Stout and I off-loaded his supplies, and then we drove the wagon beyond the pens into an open pasture and unhitched the horses. There was still some light as I neatly piled the harness sets.

"Whatever do you imagine was wrong with him?" I asked.

"Brackett?"

"Yes, he looked sick on the end."

"You didn't know?"

"No, ma'am." I stepped over to help her hobble the team. "What was wrong?"

"He was trying not to laugh out loud when you said you were going to be ranching here."

"What's so funny about that?"

She stood up and placed her hands on her hips and then stretched her back muscles. Stout placed a hand on my shoulder and slightly rocked me as we faced each other.

"It just must be the way you talk, Locke, but there are times I can't see why someone as educated as you are would ever want to be a rancher in this godforsaken land of ours."

"I'm that strange, am I?"

"Not to me." She pursed her lips tight together, still

ahold of my shoulder. "But see, the last days I've grown accustomed to you. I guess they will too."

"Lord, I hope so, Stout. I really do hope so because I'm as serious as I can be about ranching here."

She nodded and let her arm drop. I wondered how I must prove myself—there had to be a way to do that—to show them I meant to be one of their kind.

CHAPTER

8

The road wound around the base of a steep pine-covered mountain. A flat, grassy land stretched to the south. We were headed west on the final day of our journey. Stout had pointed out to me that her family's place was at the base of the round mountain ahead. We'd been without words most of the day. Neither one of us knew what to say.

"I can pay for my own keep," I finally said, trying to think of a way to stay around her and to also learn more about ranching. Certainly, nothing I'd planned to tell her sounded good enough to say as the final hour approached. I could buy myself a horse and ride somewhere. But there was no town nearby, she'd said. I couldn't believe there were people and no community.

Her elbow to my ribs was sharp. "You haven't heard one word I said, Locke McTavish!"

"I was feeling sorry for myself."

Stout blinked at me and frowned. "Are you serious?"

"Yes, I figure when we get to the gate to your ranch you'll stop these horses, throw my grip and things overboard, and shove me off after them."

Stout reined up the team. "Whoa. Listen here, I've taken the rawhiding of my life from that dang Charlie Brackett over you. Lord knows who else knows about you and me. I can't say for sure what I feel about you, but I said I'd help you get started ranching, and by gawd, I will do what I said I would unless you lost your guts for the notion."

"I haven't lost one thing. Homestead, send for a brand, what else do I have to do? Buy a few cows. Mother cows, you called them, and a bull. See, I've got everything you told me down in my mind. I have to learn to rope, and I must remember the branding needs to look like saddle leather on the cow's hide. There!"

Stout quickly grasped both of my sleeves, pulled me around to face her, and kissed me quickly on the mouth. "You done damn good!"

I nearly fell out of the seat. For just a moment I wanted to hold the back of my hand to my mouth and be sure it had really happened. She quickly turned to the front and set the team in a long jog.

"You're going to do all right," she said like a schoolteacher when you passed a spelling test. "I figured all I'd said had just gone on over like a big flock of geese heading for Canada."

"What about your people?" I asked. "What will they think about me coming along."

"They'll grow to like you, I figure. You ain't really

their kind but you ain't bad, and when we're all mixed together in a few days, they'll get over me having lost all my good senses dragging you in with me anyway."

The yellow stock dogs, a gyp and four trailing half-grown pups, came tearing out to greet us. They really burned a path to be the first ones to run along the wagon and bark friendly at us. I was well over six feet tall sitting that spring seat beside her—nothing could diminish my good feelings.

"That's Rattler," Stout said. "As a puppy she got bit by one and liked to have died. Hey, girl! Hey, girl, them pups are getting big, ain't they?" Rattler's answer came in shrill barks.

The long ranch house was low and set with a porch across the front. The peeled logs were dark with age. Two grown girls came out on the porch drying their hands on aprons and squinting to see who was on the seat of the wagon with their sister.

"They've got the hay done." Stout pointed to some large mounds of green-looking fodder.

"Where have you been?" the older of the two girls asked. Bright-eyed, straight-backed, she looked thinner than her older sister. I imagined she was Erv from Stout's description.

"We've had more things happen than you could ever imagine. Locke McTavish, this is my sister Erv, and that's Tate."

I saw the dark-eyed teenager come out and swing on the porch post and smile big for me. She was a very attractive young lady. After seeing both of them, I was still pleased with my first choice of the Rice girls.

"McTavish, is it? What line of work do you do?" Erv asked.

Stout cleared her throat before I could answer. "Will you let the poor man get his bearings. We've been harassed by outlaws, our camp run over by a bear, found poor Badger Jones dead in the road. He was murdered. And we had to do all those dirty dishes at Charlie Brackett's."

"Oh, no," Tate moaned. "Glad I missed doing those dishes of his again."

"Well, Tate, I'm sorry, and I'm sorry to you too, Locke McTavish. I just wondered who my sister had drug in?" Erv gathered her skirts in a huff and went back in the house.

"Don't mind her," Tate said. "She's been that way ever since her intended, H. B. Bentley, went to New Mexico to help his brother." Tate took my arm and led me in the house. "It don't help either when it's one of our turns to have to stay in the house. We always get cranky, and Erv's our house mother this week."

The floor was polished to a sheen. I hated to walk across the rich yellow pine boards in my boots. The leather-willow furniture was well-kept, and even the round rock fireplace looked shined with a rag. There were rifles on the wall and coiled ropes. Despite the small windows, the lamps gave the house a warmness that I felt. Folks lived there and had pride in their existence, especially these cowgirls that hated housework, to hear them talk.

"Nice house you have here," I said to Erv as she brought a kettle of food from the kitchen.

"Have a seat. I imagine you're starved. Most men are when they get here." Erv set the pan on the table.

"Thanks, I am hungry," I said, and Tate took my hat.

"You can wash up out that door." Tate pointed to the rear kitchen door.

The pail of water and wash pan were set on a table with a sack towel on a nail nearby. I scrubbed my hands and face. I listened to a Shanghai rooster bragging and clucking to his harem out in the pens. Somewhere a calf bawled for his mother. I looked over the lots and the shed barn. This was a grand country—I needed to make my place here.

"Come on, your food's getting cold," Tate said with a smile.

"Where did Stout go?" I asked, taking a seat. She was not in sight.

"To change. She's been in those clothes a long while."

I didn't think any more about it. Tate passed me fresh yellow butter to spread on the steaming biscuits. The bread and butter would have been enough treat to eat by itself. The stew was full of meat chunks, potatoes, and vegetables. I savored each bite and told the two girls about Badger's death and read the sadness in their looks.

I wondered where their father was. I had saved a little dread over meeting him. Most prospective suitors are not easily taken in by the girl's fathers, who look for the bad points in such individuals and sometimes feel invaded by their presence.

"I see you found the food," Stout said, coming in the room. Her hair was brushed to a shine and the cord outfit she wore looked very nice. I was so shocked I stood up.

"Sit down," she said, acting embarrassed. "Have you told them about poor old Badger? I've got to write the sheriff a letter about him." Stout took a place opposite me at the table.

"Tell us about the outlaws," Tate requested.

"Go ahead, Locke," Stout said. "You can leave parts of it out."

"Why?" Erv asked sharply, standing in the doorway. "We want to hear it all. Don't put words in the man's mouth."

"It was nothing—except they spied on me taking a damn bath." Stout dropped her head and shook it ruefully. The sisters both laughed out loud. Tate even slapped the table, she thought it was so funny. I almost felt sorry for Stout.

We finished our meal and the tales all the same time. Erv served me a piece of peach pie. I looked up a little shocked and thanked her. I hadn't had any peach pie in over a year.

"That's H.B.'s favorite kind of fruit," she said.

"I'd like to meet this H.B. Why, I just know a man that likes peaches has to be a grand fellow."

Erv stared across our heads then turned, looking hurt, and left the room. I started to get up to see if I could make her feel better, but Tate and Stout shook their heads.

"She'll be fine when he gets back," Tate said to reassure me.

"Then they can fight like cats and dogs," Stout said under her breath. "Erv isn't always the happy one, but she means well."

My lessons began shortly after lunch. The rope sung, cutting the air as Tate twirled the loop over her head. The action looked easy enough. I was receiving my first lesson in how-to-rope from the youngest Rice sister. She slapped the loop on a fence post and the noose popped tight with a powerful fast jerk of her arm.

"You have to cinch it down when you catch something," she explained.

I hoped I didn't look too stupid swinging the lariat, as she called the rope. Over my head in a circular motion I held the circle round and round, but I soon hung my hat and stopped to draw a deep breath with the lariat around my shoulders.

"More force!" "Use your wrist!" "Faster!" Tate was really after me as the loop fell short and hit two feet to the side, or over the post, or under it. I soon learned that ropes coiled back like the threads on a bolt. Plus, if they were recoiled incorrectly, they really would not perform properly.

"You do this while riding horseback?" I finally asked.

"Yes, but you've got a ways to go, Locke, before we try that."

"Thanks. I'll be fine if you have chores or something else needs done."

"I know," Tate said, and gave me her best warm smile. "You don't want me setting around watching while you fumble with the lariat, right?"

"I couldn't have put it better myself. I am most grateful, though, for your efforts to show me how to do this. I think I'll get on to it in a while."

She jumped to her feet off the top corral rail and brushed the seat of her riding skirt. "You'll get it down, Locke, I know you will."

The sun set and I was still tangling up in ropes. I was almost angry. In the last of the dull twilight that seemed to stay and stay forever in this land, I was still tossing the rope—I mean "hurling the lariat"—at that damn post.

Stout came out to my place beside the pens. "Erv said to tell you she had one piece of pie left. You could have it if I could save that lariat from becoming raveled to death."

I looked at the rope in my hand. It wasn't raveling any. I doubted that if I threw it a thousand times it would ravel. What did Stout mean?

"Quit roping! You'll learn how soon enough!" she said.

I handed her the rope, realizing how sore my hands had become during this drill. I needed to become tougher a lot faster. I needed to learn how to do it like Tate did with that finality at the end of the capture, snapping that loop shut on the post with a hard, back-handed jerk.

"Where's your father?" I asked as we went toward the warm yellow light of the back door.

"Up in a line shack getting drunk. The hay's done. So he can go up there and feel sorry for himself until roundup this fall."

"Anything I can do to help?"

"Go eat that peach pie so it don't rot."

"I will, I will," I said, but my mind was still on mastering the rope procedure before roundup time. I think Stout knew that. I hoped she did. I sure wanted to impress her.

CHAPTER 9

A pink dawn creased the eastern horizon. I must have started my roping practice early because there had been a large moon out when I began. Unable to sleep, I'd crept out of the house, made friends with Rattler, and went off to the corral post to reestablish my relations with that rope.

Rattler lay down to sleep nearby, weary no doubt of watching my inability and uncoordination. As morning approached, I saw some activities at the house as the girls began to stir. I kept on roping. Rattler raised up her head like something was bothering her. She lay down again, but in an instant she was on her feet, rounding up her lazy wards at the shed and tearing out barking. Someone was coming up the road. In the golden blaze striking the open country, I could make out several riders.

I hung the rope up and hurried to the house. Who were they and what did they want?

"Who's coming?" I asked as Stout took down a Winchester from the gun rack.

"We aren't certain, but they look like a posse," Erv said from the doorway. "We're just being cautious."

"I don't blame you," I said, and went to the spare bedroom and strapped on my holster. I'd need to learn to live with that gun on my waist. She'd told me that before. I had grown complacent, feeling we were secure in this basin.

"Good morning, ma'am. Is your father here?" a man's clear voice asked outside. I bent low to look at the men on horseback through the small window on my way to the front door.

"No, he's working some cattle in the hills," Erv said.

"I'm Bishop Sellers and these men with me are local farmers. We're looking for some outlaws."

"Yes, we know who you are, Bishop," Erv said. "What's happened?"

"Yesterday two vicious men robbed one of our brothers, Dale Pierce. They also assaulted his wife. Both of the men were strangers. One was quite tall with a beard, the other a smaller man."

I stepped out on the porch and nodded. "I know those outlaws, sir. One's name is Serval Dingus, the small one is Mink Seawell. They're wanted by the law."

The tall man with the Abraham Lincoln beard and stovepipe hat frowned at me. "Are you perchance a lawman, sir?"

"No, sir. My name's Locke McTavish, but Marshal Tillman is after them for robbing an army payroll."

"Bishop Sellers." The man extended his hand and I

accepted it. "Nice to meet you, McTavish. We're after them too. I do hope you young people stay prepared to defend yourself, for we aren't sure which way they went after they left the Pierces' place yesterday."

"We appreciate your concern, Bishop. We shall do that," Erv promised him. "Thank you again for the warning, sir."

Bishop Sellers nodded to us politely. His dozen men all wore floppy hats and carried many descriptions of rifles and bird guns with double barrels. They nodded politely, too, and turned their horses away to leave.

We watched them ride out. Numbers made men braver, and righteousness had its way to succeed. I felt nauseated about those two outlaws having assaulting someone's wife, though—they definitely needed to be stopped.

"I should have shot them," Stout said quietly as we stood together on the porch watching the riders leave.

"Marshal Tillman figured they'd go due east to New Mexico. It's a shame that they're in this country," I said.

"Yes, it is. Well, what do you think now that you've met them? Those are our Mormon neighbors," Stout said.

I nodded. They could have been farmers in Illinois. They weren't in cowboy dress or garb.

"Look like agrarians to me. Where could those two hide?" I asked, still staring after the posse.

"Who?" Stout asked.

"Those killers, Dingus and Seawell."

"I don't know. Why, do you want to go look for them?" she asked me flat out.

"Yes, I would. I'd need a rifle and a horse. Could I borrow Badger's?"

"I don't know what is so secret at this time of the morning to talk so softly about," Erv loudly interrupted us, "but you two need to come inside and eat breakfast."

Stout looked rather perplexed over my request and drew in a deep breath, then she slowly exhaled like she was in deep thought. "We'd need a packhorse too."

"Oh, no, I don't want to completely ruin your reputation." I looked squarely into Stout's steel blue eyes glaring at me.

"Ruin mine," Tate said, and pushed both of us toward the table. "It's time to eat, or Erv will quit cooking if we don't get set down and started."

At the table, Stout looked about to answer me before she sat down. I could see she had something on her mind as she seated herself opposite me. "Locke and I are going to go look for those two," she announced, passing the platter of pancakes.

"They looked at you in the buff, now you're—"

Stout sharply cut off Tate's teasing. "We're doing it for Badger. Those two more than likely killed him and trailed down here after they did that. Someone needs to stop them—we will."

"What about us and the ranch?" Erv asked.

"You know how to shoot if they show up. Besides, the chores are done until roundup, Dad can go get—drunk, and . . . we can go look for those killers."

"You two aren't lawmen. What will you do when you capture them?" Erv asked.

"Citizen's arrest," I explained, "a very effective way for the informed public to apprehend criminals."

"Whew, Jesus! What words!" Tate whistled, drawing a disapproving frown from her middle sister for her swearing. "Just face it, Erv," Tate said with a swing of her empty fork, "Locke has more fancy words and ways to use them than any man we know."

"You'll need some food," Erv said like she was the mother of this group, still frowning at Tate while she continued. "I'll fix up some that you can eat on the trail. Dried apricots and apples will be good. That block of cheese you bought in Flagstaff, I'll wrap some of it in cheesecloth. We've got jerky."

The "flapjacks" on my plate, as Erv called them, were too inviting not to start on. I began to eat and let them plan the menu. The molasses syrup had a bitter tang to it but tasted thick and sweet over the rich butter. I knew it would be awhile before I enjoyed such food again. Savoring the coffee, I considered how well Stout knew this land. The pair of killers couldn't hide forever. Their cruel nature to hurt folks would bring them out if nothing else. They had to be stopped.

After breakfast, I helped Erv pack the panniers to go on the packhorse and carried them out by the corral.

"You two don't take chances and get killed," Erv started in. "I wish that H.B. was here. He'd ride with you. But he's in New Mexico helping his dang brother."

"Big troubles?" I asked.

"Heavens, I guess," Erv said, placing a small bag of flour in the box.

I could tell his absence was working on her mind a lot. I hoped this H.B. got back soon too. Maybe he'd get here before we found that pair of no-accounts and could help us. I managed to hoist the box in my arms and headed for the corral with Erv giving me more instructions than my mom ever did when I was a boy.

Stout brought up a short-tailed dun horse as I set the pannier down. He looked hard and tough. She rode a golden horse with a flaxen mane and tail. Stout's horse was broad-chested and looked like he had the power and muscle to do anything; the slope of his rump denoted speed. The animal could no doubt fly.

I found myself staring at her as she rode by me sitting astride the saddle. Most respectable women in Illinois rode sidesaddle—it didn't lower my respect for Stout, but seeing a woman riding clothespin fashion was a shock for the moment. I should have guessed that anyone that drove a wagon a hundred miles by herself rode her horse like a man.

"What color phase is her horse?" I asked.

Tate must have caught my admiration for the animal. "Dandy, ain't he? Texans call them claybanks. Messikins call them palominos. I've got you a saddle and rig up at the shed."

"Thanks. Where is Stout going?" I watched her short lope the yellow horse back out in the pastureland again from where she'd brought in the line-back dun with the striped black marks on his legs.

"To get you a real horse," Tate said, and wrinkled her small nose at some notion. "That old plug of Badger's was a personal horse he used to ride from ranch job to ranch job. You'll need a good one to keep up with Gold there."

"She calls him Gold?" I asked.

"He looks gold, don't he?"

93

"Yes."

"I figured that," Tate said, nodding her head, "she's bringing in a real one, all right. She's picked out the gray mare for you."

"A mare?" I asked. Most folks rode geldings, as neutered horses were called. I didn't know if she doubted my equestrian ability and was bringing in a gentle mare for me to ride or what. "What do you call her?"

"Lightning Mare. She's quick as a cat. You'll love her."

The hard-breathing Gold ridden by Stout came in leading the big mare. Everything about her was tall. The trim feet and long legs looked very functional. Then I realized how sleek she was. The gray mare stood over sixteen hands, and every bit of her body was built for speed. I'd seen such horses on the track in Illinois at the county fair. Not many, for they were the fleetest and only a few existed in this world—they went back to the barb horse. Her refined features, the small ears, and the dish face denoted her descending from the Godalphin Arabian's blood. These horses could run for miles without being winded. How did such horses come to be in this land?

"You still want Badger's broomtail?" Stout asked, and then smiled as I breathed into the mare's nose and worked my hands over her muzzle to acquaint her to my smell. Lightning literally danced on her hind hooves, she was so anxious to be on the move. My heart raced at the prospect of riding her.

"No!" I shouted to Stout. "I want her. She's a horse of kings."

"She'll be a handful," Stout warned, still looking with a question at me.

"I want her," I yelled, and led the flighty animal to the shed on the run. Tate was supposed to be fixing a saddle for me to ride.

I brushed the dust from her back and curried out her mane and wiped her legs clean. I knew polo players who would have killed to own such an animal. Steeplechase hunters would have paid fortunes for her spirit. Little doubt she could soar over any fence or water obstacle.

I placed the saddle pad carefully on her withers, then got the saddle positioned and cinched tight. Lightning danced about while I checked the girth for tightness. Her high spirit did not diminish my desire to ride her. My God, what a horse.

Erv and Tate roped down the canvas cover over the dun horse's pack. I tied my duster and bedroll on behind the cantle with the saddle strings. Just in case we needed it, I put an extra lariat on the saddle, too, besides the tether rope.

"Here," Stout said, returning from the house with her spurs jingling. She handed me a Winchester rifle in a leather holder to buckle on under my stirrup. "We may need it if we find those scorpions."

Scorpions, I knew, were small vermin with crablike features and a curved tail that could sting you. I guess her allusion suited the pair. Mentally, I checked what I'd packed, extra socks, a towel, a spare pair of underwear, and some kerchiefs in the saddlebags, along with a razor, soap, hairbrush, and small looking glass. The box of .44 cartridges was going with me too.

Erv was listing out loud the contents of the packs as she ran to give Stout the lead rope. Like a mother hen, Erv called out this and that as Gold impatiently circled around. Satisfied that Stout was waiting for me, I prepared to mount Lightning Mare.

My left foot was in the stirrup and I swung up. The reins were in my fist. Lightning exploded into the air. With her head between her front legs, the mare left out bucking for the sky, bawling like a wild sow. Her hind feet kicked out every time she sprung off them, tossing me about in the saddle like a gunnysack filled with straw. She spun in a complete circle under me and then landed stiff-legged, ready to take off again. Then Lightning lunged into space with a force that whipped me like a rag doll.

First I lost the stirrups. They were flopping and beating my legs. I had a death grip on the horn, but the distance from the seat to my butt grew wider, and I knew I would soon be out of the saddle. Time to get off her, despite my strong feelings to the contrary.

Seated on my backside on the ground after the hard landing, I watched her go bucking off down the open grassland. I saw a flash of yellow, and I knew Stout was in fast pursuit of the gray. I slowly rose, feeling less than two feet tall, and absently brushed off my pants while watching Stout chase down the mare.

Tate caught my arm and swung on it. "She's hell the first round, but you did better than most. I bet Erv you'd never make three of her jumps."

In a few minutes, the big palomino, his nostrils flared, came huffing back with the tall gray mare in tow. Lightning's mane rippled as she half bucked and pranced along beside him on the end of her restraint. Stout handed me the reins.

"We can reconsider the whole deal. You sure you don't want to take Badger's horse?" she asked.

"Hell, no, not on your life," I said, taking the reins to the dancing gray. I turned at their cheer—Erv and Tate were applauding me.

CHAPTER
10

They might have called her the Lightning Mare. After the second time she threw me off, I had several new names for her. Most of my choices weren't for tender ears or mixed company. Three times was the charm —I finally rode her until she quit bucking. The high-spirited mare still leaped around in anticipation, anxious to be on the go.

Stout nodded she was ready. We left the Rice ranch stirrup to stirrup in a long lope. I intended to wear down this hardy gray.

"Where are we headed first?" I asked. The racing into the wind had swept my hat off my head onto my shoulders, and I really felt free aboard the powerful mare. She was one of the greatest horses I'd ever ridden.

"I want you to meet Paw. He'll be worse than a sore-toed bear, but he needs to know those two killers are on the loose up here. Besides, he can come home and look after the girls while we're gone."

"Certainly," I said, enjoying the mare in her easy run. Inside, however, I felt a big dread over finally meeting this man. Prospects are prospects, and most suitors are as wanted by the girl's father's as a polecat coming uninvited to a family reunion picnic.

"How far away is his camp?"

"We'll be there for midday. How's that?"

"Fine," I said, grateful to be riding a horse at last and seeing the country as we went.

The trail led up into the timber and we spotted some cows with calves. They were mostly whiteface with some Texas native blood, for they sported longer horns than the Durhams and even the Hereford cattle my family raised in Illinois.

"Calves are doing good this year, plenty of grass," she said, and motioned to the cattle as they slunk away. "We've got some good yearlings in the north pasture. That's where the line cabin is." She booted the yellow horse, and in a flash of his white tail, the dun, under the bulky packs, came behind her. We were going up the mountain. I was forced to duck under a low pine bough and then sent the gray after Stout and the packhorse.

Near noontime I spotted the cabin as we rode down into a great open basin. The small structure seemed to squat in the distance when we entered the wide expanse of grassland. We crossed a small stream of water and paused to lead the animals to drink.

"Good grass in this valley," she said.

I twisted in the saddle and nodded in agreement.

Actually, I was not overly impressed with the short, mostly brown forage. I had a lot to learn about Arizona pasturage. The steers and large heifers scattered across the meadowland looked up at us curiously and then resumed grazing when we passed by. There was a sheen to their mostly red and white hides, and the tongue-swirled hair on their sides told me the cattle were doing well.

"They're gaining weight. The yearlings, as you call them, are doing excellent on this grass," I said, dropping the gray in beside her. My real gnawing dread was the contents of the cabin ahead. I looked back over the large basin we'd crossed into—wide and spacious with lots of sun-cured grass these yearlings fattened so well on. It *was* a nice place to run cattle.

"What would you call them instead of yearlings?" Stout asked with a grin.

"Weaned stock, I guess. Oh, I'd call them yearlings too. I'm used to cattle with more thickness and meat qualities than these, though."

"They're getting better," she said. "A few scrub bulls on the range costs ranchers a lot. But our breeding program up here is coming. When Paw first came here the year before I was born, he and Charlie Brackett brought longhorns from Texas with them. These calves are the descendants of those Texas cows and some good Hereford bulls."

I wanted to tell her she needed some of my grandfather's great breeding-stock bulls. This wasn't the time—I was still learning about ranching in the West. There might be reasons to save my prospects, and I didn't particularly need to impress her at the moment either.

"Hello the house!" she hollered, cupping her hands to her mouth.

Nothing moved. We kept walking our horses closer and closer. I had some strong misgivings about meeting this man. He might resent his daughter going all over, unchaperoned, with me. Finally, someone ducked out the low door and squinted to see us, a big bearded man with black hair on his face—that was my first sight of Ewell Rice.

"Damn, Stout, you brought me some more whiskey?" he asked, using a hand on the low roof eaves to steady himself. Then a stern frown crossed his face. "Who in the hell is he?" Ewell took a few unsteady steps forward to better look at me.

"Who are you, boy?" he asked, raising himself upright.

"Locke McTavish, sir."

"Jesus—" Ewell Rice shook his head like he needed to clear it. "Stout, you didn't bring me any whiskey, did you?" He looked at her like he was hurt.

"Man can drink can get his own," she said.

Rice was weaving on his high boot heels and waved an accusing finger at her. "I told you that when you were little. A man had bad habits, his girls didn't need to encourage him none. I told her that—Tavish. When she was little. You ain't some damn Texas hired gun trash, are you?"

"No, sir." I recalled Stout's warning about someone assuming I might be a Texas gunhand if I wore the leather vest.

"Don't you no sir me! Boy! You sure ain't H. B. Bentley either, are you?"

"H.B. went to New Mexico to help his brother," Stout said curtly. "Dad, someone killed Badger Jones on the Mormon Lake road. They robbed that Mormon Dale Pierce and raped his wife yesterday." Stout turned to look at me with a question about the date. I agreed with a nod.

"You need to ride back to the house and keep an eye on the place until Locke and I get back," she said.

"Where in the hell are you going with him?"

"To look for those killers before someone else gets hurt."

"Damn, you a lawman?" Ewell glared at me.

"No, sir."

"Damnit, has he got a tongue to say more than yes sir, no sir, Stout? He ain't talking enough to suit me."

"Ewell," Stout said as stern as I remembered hearing her speak, "are you going to ride back to the ranch and look after things or not?"

He stood teetering on his run-down boot heels. Rice combed the black hair back with his hands again while he considered her question.

"I reckon I'll do that. This ranny here got any intentions?"

"Paw, he's a gentleman, if you're asking me." The gold horse swung around, impatient to be on the go again.

"He ain't—"

Stout cut his question off. "One of those killers is a tall one with a black beard, and a small one looks like a rat," she said. "They're snakes. Watch out for them."

Ewell nodded that he understood her, but I knew—through his whiskey haze—he was still studying me. I expected another outburst from him any minute, about how he didn't like the notion of his daughter riding off with me, but whether or not he'd broach the subject again with his daughter I wasn't sure.

"I'll saddle up and ride back home. Which way are you two going?"

"To check out the old copper mine cabin."

"Be careful, girl. The law ought to be doing this."

"I know," she said. "The law ain't here. Come on, Locke." She spun Gold around and set out west again.

I touched my hat brim in a salute, afraid that nothing had set too well between Ewell Rice and me. The gray bounded up beside her horse. She looked back and waved, then turned with a scowl on her face. Stout was in one of those burning moods when she was best left alone till she simmered down to a dull roar.

The trail narrowed, and the mountain's face turned into a steel-looking rock as we climbed the steep, single-lane path. There was country spreading out for miles below us as we went skyward. The sure-footed gray danced light on her feet. I felt the cool wind sweep my face and rubbed the beard stubble on the side of my jaw with my fist. I'd need to shave soon or the itch would have me clawing at my face.

"Dad means well," she shouted back. The echo came back three times.

"I understand," I said, and we rode on, the shoes of the horses clicking on the rock path as we climbed into the blue sky. Ewell Rice had a problem with his drinking—lots of men did in my family. For a time

I'd had the devil ahold of me, but it never solved a thing. I wanted to ranch in this grand country— sitting in a saloon would hardly be the place to learn everything I could out here.

We dismounted and let the animals blow in a saddle on top of the mountain where the smaller pines looked almost bare from the wind. We were peering down into a new land of more peaks and forests. I could hardly fathom the vastness of this unpeopled place.

"That old copper mine and cabin is down this mountain," Stout said, pointing to a spot far below us. "If they ain't there, we'll make a camp and then ride south in a wide circle tomorrow."

"Old copper mine?" I asked, curious about what she meant.

"Like a lot of diggings, it didn't pan out."

"Pan out?"

"I mean," she said gathering her reins to remount, "that there wasn't enough copper to make it worth building a road into here to get it."

"I understand," I said, and swung in the saddle. At the last moment I recalled the gray's earlier action, but she only danced around a little, and I patted her neck in gratitude.

We rode down the steep part of the trail leaning back against our cantles, the horses almost sliding as they went. Finally the trail flattened, and we looked off at a small trace of smoke.

"Someone's there," she said.

"It might not be them," I said.

"Someone could be working the mine again," she agreed.

"Guess we'll find out when we get there," I said, and booted the gray ahead of her. I wasn't hiding behind her horse's tail. Better they'd shoot at me than shoot at her.

"Don't get trigger-happy," she warned as we rode.

I felt for the handle of the new Colt. Before you've worn a holster so long it becomes a part of you, you shift it around a lot at first, then adjust it once in a while for your own comfort. I doubted I could hit a fat bull in the butt with the handgun, but it would throw lead and no one knew my skills. The fact that it was loaded and handy was some consolation.

"I won't," I promised Stout as the gray's hind feet slid under her in the loose gravel on the steep trail. Stout was right, they certainly couldn't ever make a road into this place if all the copper in the world were in this canyon.

"It's them damn Apaches!" someone shouted, and I heard the buzz of a .22 shot over our heads.

"Get down!" I shouted to her. "They're shooting a twenty-two at us."

"Where are you going?" she screamed.

I'd already spurred the gray down the mountain, the Colt in my hand. The mare made some great lunges, and then she landed on the flatter ground. We burst through some thin pines, and I spotted a white man loading a small rifle.

I fired the Colt in the air and reined in the gray. "Hold that fire or prepare to die!"

He blinked his eyes, joined by two other unarmed men in their red flannel underwear on the porch in front of the shack.

"Who are you?" the man with the small rifle asked.

"Locke McTavish, a cowboy looking for cows," I lied. "Who the hell are you?"

"Cook Brothers. I'm Able, that's Mack, and he's the kid, Dewayne."

"Tell them to get dressed," I said with a toss of my head, "there's a lady coming with me."

"A lady!" the two shrieked in disbelief and rushed inside like they were naked.

"Who are they?" Stout asked under her breath as she rode up beside me.

"The Cook brothers, so they tell me. Two of them went to get their clothes on."

"What were they doing without them on?" she asked in a stage whisper.

"Lord, Stout, I'm not certain about their habits of dress. They thought they were all alone up here, I imagine."

The two came outside wearing shirts and pants, so I booted the gray to move in close.

"We ain't seen no cows around here," Able said.

"Some times they drift this far," I said to settle the matter. "You haven't seen two men ride through have you?"

"Nope, all we seen was Injuns. Two or three bucks tried to steal some of our supplies a couple days ago. We were working in the mine, and when we came out to get something, they were helping themselves to our things."

"Apaches?" Stout asked. She frowned and turned in the saddle searching around.

"Looked like them. I shot at them but guess they hauled off their dead," Able said.

"With that twenty-two?" I asked. "You killed some Apaches with that gun?"

"Oh, yeah, I'm a good shot with it." Able held up the single-shot rifle for us to view.

"I see," I said, doubting that bee stinger could even hurt a cold-blooded Apache much less kill one. "There are two men on a killing and robbing spree up here. You best be on the lookout for them."

"Ma'am," Able said, removing his floppy weathered hat that was nearly shapeless from too many rains, "we'd fix you and Mr. McTavish a meal if you'd be kind enough to grace our table. We don't get many womenfolks up here and would consider it a plumb honor to have you here to eat with us."

"Thank you," Stout said, almost blushing at his offer. "Mr. McTavish and I will take time to eat with you."

"It would sure please us," Able said, and his brothers nodded in agreement like crows on a fence line.

I stepped down and loosened the cinch on the gray. Deep in this canyon, there was a hush on the land that soothed a man's mind.

"They look harmless enough," Stout said for my ears as she undid her girth and I took the packhorse's lead. "Sure makes you wonder what men like them are thinking, coming back in this godforsaken land to work old mines that can never pay out."

"Guess they want something for nothing. To get rich quick, huh?"

"I guess," she said, and shook her head. "Probably eating our beef to subsist on up here."

"You think they might be doing that?" I asked in a whisper as we tied the horses to a picket line between two pines. The notion of someone stealing another's livestock was shocking to me, but who could tell if they were or not because of the distance and the vastness of the land. Unless you rode up on them doing it, the theft would be hard to prove. "How can you tell if it's yours?"

"If you don't choke eating it, that means it's your neighbor's beef," Stout said with a wink for me.

I looked around. I hadn't asked Stout about the guy's Indian story either. There was no sign of any Indians, and if they did see them, the Indians were obviously gone. Stout would have an answer. I busied myself unpacking the dun. Those three guys were certainly in some kind of trance over her. I saw it in their eyes. They obviously didn't get much female company up here.

When we entered the cabin, I noticed the table was all set with candles and dishes. The crockery didn't match, but it looked official. Able quickly seated Stout on the end of the plank table in the best chair I saw inside the place.

"We ain't much on finery here, ma'am," Able said, "but we were raised better than we look."

"Stout's my name," she said, and nodded she understood.

"Yes, ma'am, Miss Stout," he said.

"No, I'm Stout, my last name is Rice."

"Good, Miss Rice," he said, and backed away to excuse himself as if he had no more suitable words for her.

Dewayne, the youngest, delivered a platter of meat

to the table. It looked well-cooked and I shared a glance with Stout. The corners of her mouth were turned enough I knew what she was thinking—whose beef?

"We have venison, beans, and fresh bread," Able announced.

Stout nodded at me, then Mack managed a few polite words about Father protect us and feed us and an amen, we began to eat.

"After supper, Able and Mack are going to play their instruments if you can stay," the freckled-faced Dewayne said.

"Sure," Stout said. "What do you play?" She passed the bread plate to me. The sourdough slices were fresh, almost steaming, and the smell was rich in my nose, reminding me we hadn't eaten since morning.

"I play the fiddle and Mack plays the mouth harp," Dewayne said quickly.

"We ain't like orchestra players," Able said modestly.

"I'll enjoy it," Stout said. The Cook brothers looked relieved.

Able could actually play the fiddle quite well, and Mack's mouth harp added to the strings. Stout and I politely listened and applauded when they completed the "Virginia Reel." Then the waltz sound began to fill the cabin, and Stout nodded at me.

"Do you want to dance?"

I nearly turned the chair over getting up. The long notes of the fiddle held me in a spell as I stepped toward her, put my hand on her waist, and took her left hand in mine. Dewayne scrambled to move chairs, saddles, and packs out of our way.

We could have been on the moon. I didn't realize we weren't in a Chicago ballroom. The floor was a little rougher than marble, but who cared as I swung her around. She was the lightest girl on her feet I'd danced with in ages. Neither of us spoke, our eyes seemed to be locked on each other as I spun the two of us around the place. Candlelight flickered on her smooth suntanned face; I was spellbound.

Then the music stopped and we stood in place, still looking into each other's eyes. I heard the Cooks' applause and saw the crimson rise in Stout's cheeks. We couldn't seem to get enough of looking at each other.

"Would you be powerful mad if I asked to dance with her next?" Dewayne asked.

I was still looking in Stout's eyes like I'd just discovered her beauty. "No, Dewayne, you can dance the next set."

CHAPTER
11

Does it feel like rain to you today?" Stout asked, pouring my coffee.

I had never seen it even shower in Arizona since I'd gotten there. "Does it ever rain here?" I asked with a smile. The sky was pink with sunrise trying to peek over the last mountain. We were in our own camp down from the Cooks' claim.

"Rains about every afternoon somewhere in these mountains this time of year. It's been a little dry right here. See, summer rains bring us the fall grass we need."

I agreed with a nod while savoring her strong coffee. The rich, hot liquid cleared the cobwebs from my brain as my body reminded me of my tight muscles from either dancing most of the evening before, watching her dance with the Cooks, or the ride up there. I had obviously used some new muscles. I can't tell you how pleasant it was in the fresh, cool predawn to enjoy her cooking, fried side meat and flapjacks with molasses, the whang of the campfire smoke teasing us when the light wind shifted. Somehow, chasing killers didn't seem to be so all-consuming at the moment.

A glimpse of the sunup came over our shoulders as we worked side by side to reload the dun. I wondered if the brothers had really run off Apaches. Nice polite lads from Pennsylvania, they didn't act very tough to me. These three brothers digging for an El Dorado looked like they wouldn't be able to get out even if they found the mother lode. I glanced back at the formidable mountain towering above us. I'd be glad when we found some sign of the outlaws. They could be anywhere, and we wouldn't know until we stumbled on them—an act I considered as dangerous as all get-out.

"Where are we headed now?" I asked.

"We can cut south. There's an old cabin in the Bradley Mountains," Stout said. "We should be there by dark."

"You figure they could be denned up there?"

"I'm guessing, Locke, but we don't have any exact trace. Otherwise that Mormon bunch would have rode them down, as bad as they wanted them."

Stout tossed the rope over the canvas and quickly tied a diamond hitch over the packs. With one boot planted on the side of the pannier, she pulled the slack from the tie rope with a grunt.

I would have to learn how to tie down the panniers.

We gathered our reins and mounted our horses. The

gray perked up, but not much. I managed to keep her head up, though she danced some.

"I think she likes you," Stout said, and swept by me on Gold, leading the dun packhorse. The canvas cover was lashed down tight; it appeared to be riding solid on the dun's back.

The brothers waved their hats when we rode by and wished us luck. I thanked them. I had enough to worry about not to fret over their useless mission to develop their mine. If anyone needed luck, those boys needed a lot.

Stout led the way and we moved westward into some grassy open country. A flock of wild turkeys took wing, and I never saw such an explosion. The big birds flew with an intensity I could hardly believe. They became dots in the sky in a second.

"Have to be quick to kill one of them," she said, twisting in the saddle to look at me.

"First ones I've ever seen in the wild. Just glad I had a chance to see them," I said with a smile for her.

She nodded and rode on. I turned to study the open grassy country hemmed in by pines.

"This country," I asked, "would it make a good ranch?"

"Fair, but you sure wouldn't see your neighbors very often."

She was right. The wild turkeys would be all there were in this land besides a man and his cows. I liked the country despite the isolation, but I wondered about water. There wasn't much sign. Stout turned off to the south and rode into the timber like she knew where she was headed.

"Anyone claiming this country?"

"Not that I know about. You'd have to like those Cook brothers because they'd be your only neighbors up here."

"They weren't bad. I figure, as moon-eyed as they were over you, I'd hire you to sit around my ranch and they'd be down there doing all my work for free."

"That's your notion," she said. I could tell by how she looked ahead that I'd managed to peeve her again. I let the gray trail the dun up the side of the mountain through the trees. I was forced to duck a bough or two. The smell of fresh turpentine was thick in my nose as we headed uphill for the blue sky.

By late afternoon we had crossed two ranges, and the horses were snorting wearily as we worked up the dry wash. Boulders the size of houses clogged the dry water course that was strewn with dead logs and sticks, jams from a recent wild flood that must have easily filled the canyon to where it would have breasted the gray. I checked the cloudless sky and wondered when it would rain again in this land.

"Hear that thunder?" she asked.

I frowned, then I heard the low distant grumble.

"We need to be out of this canyon before the rain starts. It might flood us."

"Sure," I said, and booted the gray after her. In the slice of sky above, one tall thunderhead's dark gray face shone. One little fluffy cloud surely didn't make a flood. Stout found a deer trail for us to take. Single file, we scaled out of the wash and up onto the mountainside.

Wind found us first before we located any real

shelter. Sand and grit stung my face as we dismounted and stood with our horses among some large room-size rocks. I eyed the darkening sky but could still only see a piece of the storm. The cold air telegraphed the approach of severe weather to me. Following Stout's lead, I undid my canvas coat from behind the saddle and the cold wet slash caught me with my canvas duster half on. I noted the glimpse of concern on Stout's face, and I moved to stand closer to her.

Beads of ice pelted us first, and I was grateful for the felt hat. The thumbnail-size hail pecked us and the animals. It drummed on the pack cover and looked like shelled white corn on the ground at our feet. Harder wind slashed at us as we bowed our backs to the gale and huddled side by side. Thunder grumbled overhead with blinding flashes of lightning. Made we wonder why I ever asked when it rained in this land.

Then the torrential downpour quit and the gentle rain dripped down. I was cold to the bone. What now? I wondered, waiting on her cue.

"Ready to ride?" she asked.

"Next time I ask for rain, you remind me how it comes," I said.

Stout laughed as she mounted and then set Gold on up the mountainside.

The sun came out and the sky turned back to clear blue. The air quickly heated, making it hot as an oven. Freezing one minute, baking the next, Arizona Territory was proving to be a strange land. Now too hot for the coat, I strung it over my lap, not wanting to take time to tie it on the back of the cantle as we rode on.

I lifted the heavy, sodden hat and wiped my sweaty

face on my sleeve. Grateful for the fresh wind, I turned and remembered the turkeys with a twinge of being impressed all over again.

"Guess I misjudged the distance," she said. Stout wore a concerned look as she scanned the maze of mountains beneath us. We had drawn rein on top of yet another ridge line.

"Are we close to that cabin?" I asked, stretching my tight back muscles as the gray stood beside her mount.

"No," she said, looking disappointed. "I may have us completely lost. I don't see one familiar peak or mountain."

I looked around and nodded. "Oh." I couldn't tell a damn thing—I'd been lost the entire time myself.

"Is it serious?" I asked.

"We ain't getting to that cabin like I said we would."

"I'd rather be lost with you than anyone I know."

"You ain't any dang help, Locke McTavish. We better camp down there tonight, and we'll head east in the morning. We'll come out somewhere. And Locke? Whatever you do when we come out, don't say a word about us being lost, huh?"

"Oh, I won't," I said, and almost smiled. I figured Stout Rice could whip most men if they made her mad enough, but she feared being teased more than anything else in the world. I recalled my threat to tell those clerks at Babbett Brothers that we were engaged.

"I don't think it's funny at all!" she said, scowling at me as she reined the palomino around to start off the mountain.

"Considering what I know about this country, I think it's damn funny that you'd even confide in me that you were lost."

We both laughed as I rode on after her. Scrambling around boulders, we finally selected a campsite in a grove of pines beside a pool of rainwater.

"We'll need to feed the horses grain. There ain't much grass up here for a hobbled horse," she said. "Tie them on a picket line. I'm going to take a bath. I smell worse than the horses."

"Yes, ma'am," I said as she left me.

The canyon was deep and the shadows lengthened long before sundown. The horses crunched on corn in their nose bags. I chopped more firewood while I heated water to shave with on the small fire. My tongue hungered for coffee more than food.

In a short while, Stout returned with her short hair still damp. She dried it on the flour sack towel and smiled. "There's a larger hole down the wash a ways to bathe in if you want to."

"I'll go do that. You start supper," I said, and went to gather my towel. "There's enough wood cut up."

"Thanks," she said.

I grabbed a bar of soap and a towel, which I swept over my shoulder. Scrambling over and around great boulders, I adjusted the Colt out of habit. The pool of water looked very inviting. I quickly stripped off my clothes and waded into the cool water to my knees. A perfect bathtub about ten feet across, I lathered my body and scrubbed my clothing. I was so busy I barely noticed the shadows growing deeper. With my clothing rinsed, I spread them on the rocks to dry.

I spotted something shining on the ground on the far side of the pool. Curious to see what it was, I waded across the water hole.

I bent over and recovered a necklace with hammered silver coins and some green rocks threaded on the leather string. I swirled it in the water to remove the wet sand from it. It was an Indian's thing. I stood there with the cool air drying my bare skin, with the heavy necklace in my hand. The evaporation process was fast covering me with goosebumps. Quickly, I scanned the forested steep slopes above me for any sign. This was definitely Indian jewelry.

Where were they? Watching us? I needed to get my underwear on and hurry back to warn Stout. My throat felt constricted as I backed cautiously into the water holding the Indian totem in my hand like it was something unreal.

Ever try to pull wet pants over wet underwear? Nearly impossible when you're in a hurry. I cursed under my breath as I kicked my way into those sodden cord pants. My wet socks would never go in those Coffeyville boots either. So I dismissed it and decided to go back barefooted. Britches on was enough. I felt anxious about Stout being alone in camp. I hurried with my arms full of damp clothing, trying to look in all directions and expecting to see an Indian's hostile face any minute. I'd seen plenty of engravings in the press of war-painted Indians before I came to Arizona.

"What's wrong?" Stout asked, seeing me coming on my tender soles.

"Indians. Look, I found this at the edge of that big pool. One of them must have dropped it."

Stout examined the necklace, and I noticed she went to eyeing around the camp too.

"What should we do?" I asked. As a precaution, I

drew the rifle out of the scabbard and levered a shell in the chamber.

"I'm not sure. The army's rounded up most of the bad renegades. There haven't been any Apaches even passing through here in several years."

"What other kind of Indians would wear that necklace?"

"I'm not certain. They trade jewelry among themselves. But yes, it could be from an Apache. Those Cook boys swore they shot at one stealing their things." By the set of her blue eyes, Stout looked equally concerned over my discovery. My belly felt like it had a small fire in the pit of it, burning a hole through the lining. I shifted the Winchester in my hands—I wasn't hungry or tired now. I dressed in my damp shirt.

A coyote cried out with his mournful plea as darkness quickly engulfed the mountains. By Stout's own admission, we were lost. We might even be camped among some bloodthirsty savages. Clearly and mournfully, the coyote's yelping carried down the slope and raised the hair on the back of my neck. Then another pack member joined in with his howling. It would be a long night.

CHAPTER
12

In the starlight Stout stood guard with the Winchester. I finished saddling the horses in the darkness. We'd decided it was time to move on. She was certain Apaches did not attack in the night, something about their spirits going to hell if they were killed during the nighttime hours.

"You'll have to tie the hitch over the packs," I said, and took the rifle from her. Nothing moved, but the night insects were chirping. The only other sound was the gentle hushing wind in the pine needles on the slopes.

I wondered if she could find our way in the night. We didn't need a special route, just any way to get out of these jumbled-up mountains. Before I found that necklace, being lost didn't even seem serious to me. In fact, the situation had been funny. Who cared, I was seeing the country and enjoying being alone with her.

Though I wanted those two outlaws stopped before they hurt someone else—finding the Indian necklace changed lots of things for us. Was there only one or were there a hundred redskins in the area?

"I've got it done," she said softly. "You lead the dun horse, I'll pick the way. Gold will get us out of here. Remember, you can always let the dun go if we get in a running war or something and have to really run for our lives."

I grunted to acknowledge that I heard her, but I wasn't letting some damn Indians have that dun horse and all our possessions. They'd have to kill me first. I swung up on the gray, and the mare acted civilized for the first time as if she understood what dangers were at hand. The dun came along easily. By the silver starlight I could make out the gold horse's flaxen tail and form easily, maybe too easily.

We were forced to stick close to the wash due to the steep slopes. The skin on my neck crawled as we wound our way downhill. I knew the clack of the horses' iron shoes must be echoing across the entire mountain. Surrounded by giant boulders in the shadowy darkness, I had to let the gray follow Stout.

Above me on the rock there was movement, and I glanced up to see what it was. A shadow loomed. I thought for a moment it was an owl that had spread its wings, but then it leaped for me. No owl, the blood-curdling scream drew the cords tight in my neck. The force of the attack tore both of us from the saddle. I barely had time to issue Stout a warning to look out.

The ground was hard. A sharp pain in my side told me my ribs must be cracked from striking a rock in the fall. All the air was out of my lungs as I kicked the smoke-stinking, wiry Indian away. There were cries and gunshots. Stout was cursing in the night. The horses panicked at the shooting at close quarters. I barely rolled away in time to avoid being stomped by the prancing gray, but it gave me a few precious seconds.

Where was my attacker? I fought to raise to my knees and draw the Colt at the same time. The hammer hung in the holster by the small rawhide thong. I finally freed it. The Colt filled my hand and I remembered to cock it. The attacker charged me with a nerve-shattering cry. The cherry red explosion of the blazing black gunpowder went off in his teeth-bared face at my arm's length. The shot was deafening.

His steel blade knife still ripped my shirtsleeve as he swung around, and the keen edge tore at the skin and flesh of my left arm. I fired another round into him as he reeled back. The Indian pitched into the darkness, and I whirled to snap a shot at a second figure poised on the rocks above me. He vanished. Whether I hit him or not I was uncertain.

"Stout! Stout!" I shouted, scrambling to my feet, wary every moment a second brave would spring on me. "Are you all right?"

"I'm fine. Are you hurt?"

"No. How many more are there? I thought these devils did not attack at night."

"I'm not sure now. They must have new rules."

I glanced back in the direction of the wounded or dead Apache, too dark to see a damn thing clearly. I could not detect a single sound, but my heart was raging so loud I felt certain every Apache on the mountain could hear it. My breathing came deep and hard.

In a low crouch I moved carefully toward Stout's location. My ears hurt from straining for a sound. I noticed my left sleeve was wet with something sticky —blood. The Apache had taken a toll on my limb. I disregarded the wound.

When I reached her place behind a large rock, I had a little trouble ejecting shells with my hurt arm, holding the barrel up as I pushed out the casings with the ejector rod.

"What happened to you?" I asked, trying not to let her see my wound. It would quit bleeding after a while. I pressed my back to the rock, keeping that arm away from her. I jammed new cartridges in the cylinder.

"Two of them jumped out of nowhere and grabbed Gold's bridle. I went to shooting at them. Another jumped off the rock to tackle me, but he missed me because Gold was plunging around."

"Did you kill any of them?" I asked.

"I wounded two, I think, but they left. The one who hit the ground left, too, with the horses milling all around. I think the dun kicked him pretty hard. He kicked someone solid. I heard it."

"My Injun's dead. I shot at another up on the rocks." I tossed my head in that direction. "You reckon they got our horses?"

"Probably. I got off Gold to come help you, and the horses went on down the mountain during all the confusion."

"Damn, I'm sorry, Stout," I said, feeling depressed over not handling the attack with more authority.

"I'm the one got us lost."

"Guess we better stay here till daylight so we can see them?" I reached over and squeezed the hurting arm.

"Yes. What's wrong with your forearm?"

"I scratched it."

"Let me look." Stout took hold and turned it to the starlight. "Why, damn, Locke McTavish, you've cut it real bad."

"No."

"You're bleeding like a stuck hawg," she said, jerking the kerchief off my neck and wrapping the forearm so tight it hurt worse. Then she tied hers around my neck for a sling.

I settled my butt on the ground as she fussed over the cut.

"If we walk out, how long do you figure it will take us to get there?" I asked.

"Might take a week," Stout said. "East is the only way I know to go."

"Daylight, we'll do just that very thing. Damn, I hate those red devils taking your good horses."

"Me too. But do you know why I hate it so much?"

"I guess I do." The arm began to throb and every breath hurt my chest. Then I remembered the ribs and decided I better not let her know about them.

"No, you can't even imagine what they'll do with those good horses."

"What's that?"

"They'll eat them." Stout shook her head ruefully. "Damn Apaches would rather eat a horse as anything."

"Oh, my God." I couldn't believe even an Apache

would do that, but that was thinking like I would, appreciating the quality those horses represented in a world of plugs and nags.

"I think they've gone," I said, wanting to start moving. My arm would not get better sitting on my butt, and the dull ache was increasing. In a few hours it would really be hurting. My ribs felt like I had a bad case of indigestion. I didn't want to hold her back.

"Sit for a minute," she said.

"Why?"

"I'm worried I have nothing to put in that cut of yours to clean it. You might get blood poisoning."

"What should we do?" I asked, trying to shake the pain and control the anxious feeling I had inside me to get moving.

"We better build a fire and sear it."

I frowned at her idea. "Are you serious?"

"Serious as I've ever been. I don't want you to die."

"Neither do I, but I'll be fine without doing all that."

She shoved me back down. "Sit still and let me think what I should do."

"We need to get moving," I insisted.

"No! Those Apaches have our horses and supplies. They'll hightail it somewhere else. That's what they do—hit and run. They've got what they wanted for now."

It was useless for me to consider arguing with her. She had her mind set and that was it.

Stout crept around gathering small bits of drift-wood and made a small fire in a bowl she hand-dug in the sand. I kept the Colt handy. I began to doubt

I could even swing the long-barreled Winchester around if necessary.

She took my jackknife to heat the blade since that was all we had to use to sear the cut.

"This may hurt bad," she said, unwrapping my arm and placing it on a flat top of a rock. "Wish I had a needle and thread to sew that up. It's going to leave a big scar." She shook her head. "Just you bite down on something."

I took a bite on the scarf she'd put around my neck. My teeth were set, for I figured the searing would certainly hurt like hell.

Using both her gloves to hold it, she brought the jackknife from the fire. I bit down on the scarf knot, and the scorching smoke was bad as she applied the red hot blade to my knife wound. The stench of burning flesh ran up my nose and made my eyes water. The wound sizzled under the hot metal as she pressed down.

My knees buckled despite my effort to stand, and I collapsed as she set the knife aside.

"Hey, hey, what are you doing?" she shouted, but I was already fainting.

No one ever dies from being cut in the arm. But I figured I was in the land of the hereafter when I awoke. My arm ached hard and deep. It may have woken me—the pain, that is. Sunlight flooded in my eyes. I could barely see out of one eye at a time. Stout stood above me holding the reins to the gray mare.

"Lightning came back. They must have tried to ride her and she threw them," Stout said, excitement written on her face as she helped me stand. I bobbed a little and finally got steady on my feet. Breathing was hard to do. Those ribs were knifing me inside as bad as the arm hurt on the outside. "She came back to us, anyway."

"That mare wasn't stupid. She didn't want to be supper, I guess," I said as she swung up. Stout removed her foot from the stirrup so I could get up behind her. My left arm wasn't working, so Stout had to help me up behind her with some effort. My bedroll made it a high seat, but who cared? I settled down, grateful to be riding instead of walking. In the shape I was in, it certainly beat walking. She had the Winchester back in the scabbard under our legs. I reached behind myself to reset my holster.

"Easy, Lightning," she scolded as the gray pranced.

"All I need is to be thrown off," I said, using my good arm to hold onto Stout's waist so I didn't fall off. I closed my eyes thinking how nice this position would be if I didn't hurt so. I had my girl in my arm. The jarring of the horse caused me to catch my breath, and I realized riding would not be the most pleasant mode of travel.

"What's wrong?" she asked.

"Nothing," I managed. She didn't need to worry about my ribs. We needed to get the hell out of those mountains.

"I know you're hurting, aren't you?" she asked. "Hang on. We'll be on level ground soon. I think Lightning came back for you."

"Oh, good. Don't worry about me."

The Indians must have become absorbed into the land. Though I repeatedly twisted and turned with pain-filled movements to look for them as we rode east, there was no sign any Apaches had ever been in there. No sign of Gold or the dun horse either.

In the level country, the riding went better. I could bend over and hold my side sitting atop the bedroll and cushion some of the hurt in my ribs. I tried to hide it from her.

"I know where we are," she said near noontime.

"Good," I barely managed. My head was swimming. I never knew exactly when I became unconscious and fell off the horse. I heard Stout scream. Were there more Indians? I was no help to her. I was in Illinois racing a buggy against a school classmate again. Thurman's pacing mare was stout and she could really pace, but I was in the lead. The black horse was grandfather's best, and I was using the whip handily. Then we crossed a small wooden plank bridge and the black went down, the buggy flew through the air, throwing me into the rail fence. I recalled the pistol shot that awoke me when Grandfather destroyed the black horse.

"His leg's broke, laddie." I remember the sadness in Grandfather's heavy face and the snow white eyebrows that furrowed over his deep-set blue eyes. "Nothing else we could do for the black. Lucky you're alive. Your friend Thurman—he was killed, too, you know. Sorry, laddie, but horse races ain't all winning now, are they?"

"No, Grandfather."

In my nightmare, they shot the horse again and again. I must have been screaming for Stout. I awoke and she held my head in her lap. She looked very concerned.

"They shot the black horse. He broke his leg, you know?" I asked her.

"Yes, be calm. You fell off the gray mare from behind me. I think you're some delirious. Did anyone ever tell you have a terrible Scottish accent when you're like that too? I could barely understand you."

"I was dreaming of a horse and buggy race with a friend named Thurman Walters that ended in a wreck. He was killed."

"Did you remember hollering 'No, Thurman' to me?"

"Not really," I said, and struggled to sit up. Not that I did not enjoy the comfort of her legs as a pillow and her generous nursing, but we needed to get out of this country. I felt certain the Apaches would return.

"You ride in the saddle, if you can. I'll ride in back. We'll use the bedroll to help hold you in the seat. Or else I'll make a travois and haul you back to the ranch."

"I'll make it in the saddle," I said and rose, pushing off my knees. The sharpness inside my ribs sawed at me as I tried to straighten, then I realized Stout was holding me up.

"Sure you will," she said. "Can you stand while I get the gray? She's over there grazing."

I blinked my eyes. I couldn't see her. I mean I couldn't even see where Stout went, though her voice sounded not twenty feet away. Damn! I was busted up inside, my arm nearly cut off and I was going stone blind. All I could see was light and darkness and things close up.

She held the horse. I made out a fuzzy outline as I felt with my good hand for the cantle to mount up.

Stout's shoulder under my butt boosted me into the saddle. The saddle horn gouged my ribs as I was flung over it in the effort to mount. I saw stars. This was depressing.

"Here," she said, fussing over locking my legs under the bedroll and tying it down. "You can ride like a dead man now and stay on."

Stout probably was right, I felt like I was dying. She mounted behind me and reined the gray with her hand in front of me. Several times she righted me when I grew woozy. The sharpness of her tug usually woke me enough to ride on some more.

"It's a toss-up where we should go, but I think that we'll head for McFee's. He's the best home doctor we've got in the country."

"How far is that from here?"

"Oh, not far. I know where we are now." Stout spurred the gray into a short lope. She leaned against my back to reach forward to give the mare some rein, and I nearly blacked out. With the saddle horn clutched in the deathlike grip of both hands, I figured I'd break into smaller pieces since I couldn't fall out as a whole body.

CHAPTER

13

"You girls give me a hand," Barney McFee said as he started to ease me off the gray horse onto his shoulder.

My groan forced him to stop.

"What's wrong?" he asked.

"Broken ribs, I think," I said through my teeth.

"Here, I'll help," Stout said. "He really fought off those red devils—" The world went hazy as their strong arms lifted me off the saddle.

Next I knew, I was on some bed and McFee was shouting for a scissors or knife. I could see the outline of Stout standing above me. Then I felt the cold blade of a scissors sliding over my skin and maybe the back side of a knife cutting away too at my underwear. Damn, McFee was going to undress me right before those two girls.

"Here, laddie, have some whiskey." He held my head up and pressed the bottle to my mouth. "This

131

business is going to hurt you some, but I must bind up those broken ribs."

I wanted to protest about being naked. I wanted to tell them there was no need in all this fussing over me, that I'd heal, but the whiskey cut off my protest and I was forced to swallow it. The liquor was strong enough to flush tears from my eyes. We hadn't eaten since God knew when, and I realized the whiskey would kick me like a mule when it reached my empty stomach.

The two girls scrubbed the skin off my chest and arms. Then they rolled me over, scrubbed my back, and dried me. Next I knew they were powdering my skin with corn dust. The powder had some kind of perfume in it. Though I was groggy, I could smell the flowery aroma. I'd probably die and go to hell smelling like some high-priced dove. That perfume smell would be hard to explain to Satan or his helpers. I could plead innocent till the milk cows came home, and who'd believe me? It hurt me too much on the inside to even think about laughing.

"You've got to sit up so I can bind your ribs," McFee said in my ear. "Can you do it, lad?"

"Yeah," I grunted, and with my head swimming, I started to raise up. Strong arms helped me until I was seated on the edge of the bed, out of wind and exhausted.

"How high can you lift your arms?" McFee asked, almost in my face. I could only make out part of his jawline, my vision was so hazy.

"Not much," I said, dreading the thought of the pain if my elbows even left my side.

"Girls, help him," he said.

I could hear myself scream in the distance when the girls raised my arms. The pain in my chest felt like a dozen lances jabbed through me. McFee talked a hundred miles an hour about how this wrapping my chest would only hurt for a little while and it would be so much better afterwards.

The lamps had rings around them like a foggy moon as I tried to focus and see them. I was, for all purposes, blind. I couldn't have whipped a baby. McFee really tightened down on his wrapping and I caught my sharp breath.

Later I awoke to Stout's voice, not sure what Stout had first told me. She was seated on the edge of the bed. I was fairly drunk from the rest of the whiskey he poured down me so I'd sleep. They had piled quilts on me to sweat some of the poison out of my system.

"Can you hear me, Locke?" she asked.

"Yes," I managed, shocked at the dryness in my voice.

"I'm going to ride over to home and check on things. McFee ain't seen those two around here. I want to be sure Dad came down to stay with Erv and Tate. You just rest, all right?"

I nodded.

"And Locke, I meant what I said. You sure were brave up there taking on those Indians. You'd do to ride with to hell and back." She straightened to her feet; it rocked the bed a little and the movement pained me. I listened for her because I'd never opened my eyes. She didn't need to know I was blind. If she could see my eyes were milky, or whatever they were like, she might feel more sympathy for me. I didn't want that.

Then I felt her breath on my face, and to my shock she kissed my lips. It was a small, quick kiss, but it meant a lot to me. It may have been the best one in my entire life. I also realized how crusted and split my lips had become. Still, I didn't open my eyes. She didn't need the burden of my blindness on her conscience.

"You watch out for yourself," I managed to croak out.

"I will. Don't talk now. You get some rest. I'll be back tomorrow evening. I may take your carcass to a real doctor in Flagstaff if you ain't doing a lot better when I get back."

"Yes," I said in agreement. I wanted to see her but I didn't dare open my eyelids. I heard her boot heels clunk across the floor and heard her whisper good-bye to me from the doorway. Sleep wanted me and I quickly slipped into a sound nap.

My pores opened up while I slept. I woke in a sea of sweat. My throat felt like someone had taken a horseshoe rasp to it. Behind my temples, a raging hammer pounded. The room was pitch dark and the house quiet. I finally managed to escape into sleep again. Several times I awoke, groggy and dizzy. I knew I must have broken the fever for I felt almost cool and clammy under the tower of blankets. I even removed some of the quilts and let them fall on the floor, for it was way too hot under the load.

A rooster crowed. I heard McFee's jersey cow bawl to be milked. The ranch was astir. Even a pig or two squealed for breakfast. I looked at the beams overhead as the first light of morning shone in the small window over my bed.

I could see! Thank you, God! I blinked my scratchy eyes over and over as I jubilantly studied the underside detail of the brown shingle roof, cobwebs matted in the small spaces. I could see and I was going to be all right. A miracle! Where was Stout? Gone home. I wondered if I should have let her do that by herself.

I needed to get up and empty my bladder. I swung my legs out, grateful they'd at least left me the bottom half to my long handles. The effort to sit up was filled with sharp pain inside McFee's bindings. I wasn't completely healed. The world tilted a little when I pulled on my pants. Normally, I'd put my shirt on first, but in this case I worried about being able to reach down and get my pants on.

Beads of sweat ran down my face, but I managed to get my pants up. I didn't need the shirt, and pulling on my boots was out of the question.

I drew a deep breath and then rose stiffly to my bare feet. The back door couldn't be far. I might not make the outhouse, for I certainly felt light-headed. When I slumped against the door facing and squashed my limb, the bandaged arm began to throb. I could see the rear door and decided McFee and his daughter must be outside doing morning chores.

In the kitchen I used a ladderback chair to brace myself on while I caught my breath. Bent over, I rested for a moment, letting some of the deep hurting in my ribs subside. Through the back window I noticed two horses and riders coming out of the timber. It was a strange direction for riders to come to a place. They kept twisting around, looking like they were checking on everything.

The two outlaws, Dingus—with his matted black beard, and the small one with his weasel look— Seawell, were only a hundred feet away from the back door of the cabin. They were coming in the back way to harm McFee and his daughter! I turned too quickly and the pain shot through my body as I nearly fell to my knees. I hoped the Colt was in that room. I didn't know where any of McFee's guns were. Something had to be done, and I was the only one that could do anything. I quickly realized Barney McFee never packed a pistol about the place.

I lurched down the hallway like a drunk bouncing off the wall to keep from falling. Finally, in the doorway to the room and out of breath, I tried to focus on the table by the bed. My vision swam, and I worried the blindness was returning. So dizzy I could hardly stand, I staggered forward and pitched myself belly down on the bed to save hitting the floor. There were killers outside in the yard. Folks needed help, and I was weak as a baby. The muscles in my legs were shaking; even gritting my teeth didn't help.

I managed to roll over, then sit up with my molars locked tight against the raging fire inside my upper body. The Colt was on the nightstand. I undid the rawhide loop and slid the heavy pistol out. The revolver felt like it weighed a ton. I pushed it in my waistband and rose as slowly as possible to avoid any jarring.

Each step I took toward the doorway was hard fought. The lightness in my head mixed with the jarring headache, made me wonder if I could even see to shoot at them.

Sharp voices close by in the yard made me stop and catch my breath and bearings.

"You better go get us all your money or you'll never see this girl again, old man!" Serval Dingus ordered.

"You touch a hair on that girl's head, and I swear I'll break you in two with me bare hands!" Barney threatened them.

"Listen, you won't be so damn tough, old man, when we get through with you!" That was Mink's voice.

My shoulder rested on the wall to steady me. I went toward the front of the house a few small steps at a time. I wanted to be in a front room chair to face them. Then all I'd need to do would be to cock and fire the pistol if they didn't give up.

They were coming to the house. My time would be short. I needed to be in the living room when they came in so I could cover them. Twenty steps, maybe less.

"Father, do as they say!" Kathreen McFee screamed, and I looked to the front door, expecting them any second. It had been left open. I had maybe ten steps more to go to reach the chair of choice.

I took a deep breath and half ran to seat myself in the high-backed rocker. It took a moment for the world to stop spinning. I drew the Colt from my waistband, cocked the hammer, and waited.

Then Dingus shoved McFee through the open door. On his heels, Mink roughly pushed the girl through the doorway. They hadn't even seen me, they were so busy looking all around for any threat.

"Throw your hands in the air! Fall down, Kathreen!" I shouted and leveled the Colt at Mink.

Wide-eyed, she bent over as if on cue, and I fired the Colt. My aim was high over her head, but the bullet intended for Mink went wild. The black powder smoke billowed up, fogging the room. Mink turned in cowardly fashion and ran out the front door. Kathreen screamed at the top of her lungs, rattling the window glass.

I stood up, unable to see the taller outlaw and her father, but I could hear the two men struggling in the hallway. Someone hit the floor with a thud. On her knees, Kathreen screamed for her father to watch out.

I finally reached the hallway, gun ready, but knew I was too late when I heard the sounds of the back door being jerked open. The girl was on her knees pleading with her father who was lying on the floor. I aimed at the fleeting figure of Dingus as he exited the back way.

The gunsmoke from my second shot billowed up and fogged the entire house in a blue haze. I heard Kathreen and McFee coughing. Those were good sounds—if they could cough, they were alive. The noise of the outlaws mounting horses outside wasn't pleasant. The very thought that they were escaping again depressed me.

"We'll get you, pilgrim. Next time, I'll blast your ass away!" Dingus swore.

Pistol shots shattered the front glass panes, but I

was unscathed standing across the room holding the butt of my Colt so hard I knew I must be squashing the hard rubber grips. Those two would pay for this.

"We'll get you the next time, pilgrim!" Mink added, and then they hurrahed their horses and left in a clatter of hooves. Two final shots at the house punctuated their threat, and they rode off to the north.

"You two all right?" I asked. My knees were about to buckle. With my back against the wallpaper, I let myself slowly slide down the wall into a sitting position on the floor.

"We'll be fine, but you should be in bed, man," McFee said, worried.

"I thought he had killed you," I said, looking at the man.

"Just hit my hard head with his pistol barrel. Probably bent the damn gun, he did."

"Hard to kill a Scot, isn't it?" I smiled at the two of them.

"You saved our lives, lad."

"Yes you did, Locke. Why they would have . . ." Kathreen slowly shook her head and chewed her lower lip at the prospect of being taken by the outlaws. "It was a miracle you were here. I don't know what we'd have done."

"Guess I've earned me a drink of whiskey," I said, feeling uneasy about Kathreen thinking my clumsy actions were so great. I'd nearly bungled it up. One thing for certain, I needed the whiskey to numb the hurting. I'd torn something loose inside, and it really stabbed me. The sharpness made my breathing sound like a stuttering man talks, a short gasp at a time.

"You're damn right. You can have all I've got, lad.
Go get him a bottle, Kathreen."

Her green eyes looked at me hard, then in a flurry of
petticoats and gathered-up skirt, she left us.

"You should never have got out of bed," McFee
said.

I nodded. I still had a pressing bladder, only it was
worse than before. I would have to get McFee to help
me. Damn. That was the height of helplessness for me.

CHAPTER

14

No sign of them," Stout said, swinging the tail of her lariat and slapping the bullhide chaps she wore. "We've rode everywhere. Everyone in this country is out searching for them and the Indians. The Apaches must have gone back to the reservation. And those two outlaws can't hide forever."

The sun warmed me in the big rocker McFee brought out on the porch for me to sit in. There was a quilt over my legs on day three of my recovery. Barney thought the poison was out of my wound, but the ribs would take time to heal. My strength was returning much slower than I liked.

Every rancher and dirt farmer in North Cut had been alerted and was watching for signs of the outlaw pair. Many small groups rode by the McFee place in their search and stopped to visit. Even the bishop gave me a thank-you for my effort.

"Where could they go south?" I asked Stout, using the side of my hand to shield against the sun's glare.

"After Linter's store, it's awfully broken country." Stout frowned at me. "I thought you said they rode north from here?"

"That might have been what Dingus wanted us to think. He could have circled back."

Stout nodded and placed one of her boots on the porch. She rested her wadded-up gloves on her knee. She arched her back against tired muscles, for I knew she'd spent the better part of the past three days in the saddle.

"I'll be able to ride tomorrow," I said. "We'll go look that region over. Besides, no one has seen those Apaches either. I'd certainly like to get Gold back for you."

"As much as I wish you could find him, I doubt we'll ever recover Gold. Besides, Barney won't let you go riding off."

"He's not my mother. In the morning we'll saddle up and ride south."

"What will you ride?" Stout glanced up at me.

"The bald-faced horse you brought up here three days ago."

She tried to suppress her grin. "How do you know that's for you?"

"I saw you lead him in all saddled the other day. I figured you intended for me to ride him. That was why you brought him along."

"But I don't think . . ."

"Stout Rice, are we going together or do I have to go alone?"

She hooded her eyebrows in a frown and glared at

me. "Together, I guess. Someone will need to keep the buzzards from eating your ornery hide when you pass out and fall off that horse."

"I've only fainted twice in my life."

"You'll do it again if you try leaving here too soon."

"It's a chance I'll take."

She inhaled through her nose and then pursed her lips in disapproval. "You need to take it easy for the rest of the week."

"Those outlaws will be in kingdom come, or worse than that, they'll hurt someone else."

Stout agreed and left me to put up her jaded saddle horse standing hipshot by the shed.

I dozed in the chair, the Colt handy in my lap. I would never go anywhere without my firearm again, not until Dingus and Seawell were locked behind bars.

Thunder woke me. I could see some fat rain clouds were drifting in our direction. Rain swept down the south slope, and soon drops began to pelt the porch roof and run off the eaves. The thunder grumbled louder and the spray was reaching my face.

"Why, it's storming hard. Come inside, Locke," Kathreen McFee said, rushing out the doorway. "I'll get the chair for you."

"I hate for a woman to have to tend to my things," I said, rising slowly and letting the complaints in my chest dissolve before I moved to the front door.

"No problem. I overheard you talking to Stout. I just wondered . . . have you spoken for her?"

"Not really, but I plan to."

"Oh."

"Why?" I asked as she dragged the rocker over the rough boards and inside the front door.

Another wave of drops thrown by the strong winds struck my face as I took a last look at the downpour that obscured the corral and sheds. Stout must have been caught at the saddle shed caring for her horse. I guessed it might pour for some time.

Kathreen shifted her dress waist around straight and smiled at me. "I just wondered if anyone else had a chance to interest you?"

"I've got a cousin, Kathreen. He's four years younger and a lot better looking than I am. Norman might come out here to meet you someday."

"You're saying what you have for Stout is permanent."

"Yes, ma'am," I said, feeling a little uneasy to be pinned down by another girl about my intentions.

"I'd like to meet this Norman if he's like you." Kathreen smiled openly and turned to leave me.

"I'll write him and tell him to come see North Cut and meet my good friend Kathreen McFee."

"Do that!" Kathreen gathered her skirt and left me. I felt relieved at her departure as I eased down on the rocker. She had been a very sincere nurse, and I owed her more than a polite thank-you.

Out the open door I watched the shafts of water pouring onto the yard outside. Cold wind even found me in the house, and I was forced to use the quilt for a coat as I studied the hard rain. Stout might never agree to marry me. I hadn't asked her, but the notion seemed central to my thoughts as I lounged around like I was sick, rather than just plain weak.

Thunder struck close by and rattled the whole house. Stout, with rain dripping off her hat, burst in the door. She grinned at me and shook her short hair as she removed her soggy hat.

"Wet out there, Locke."

"It sure is. Rains somewhere in these mountains everyday, they tell me." I knew while listening to her laughter and watching her back as she hung up her slicker I'd have to ask for her hand—one of these days.

Morning came as bright as a Fourth of July Chinese firecracker. Stout busily saddled both horses. Stout told me in short words before she left the house she'd ready our horses and for me to stand back. I ambled around while she worked.

The cool wind swept down the valley. I noticed Kathreen in what I guessed was her best blue dress. She was returning from milking the cow, the wooden pail in her hand.

"You sure this is what you want to do?" Stout asked, reaching under for the back girth on the bald-face horse.

"I'll be fine. You won't have to nursemaid me."

"Fine! Whoa, Baldy," Stout said in soft command, and the cow pony settled down. "He's all right," she said, straightening. "I picked him 'cause he's Dad's 'get drunk' horse. He always manages to bring Dad home no matter the condition."

"I appreciate that."

Stout looked toward the house. McFee was calling us for breakfast. "Nothing says we can't call this off and let you mend another day or, better yet, the rest of the week."

"I'll be fine once I get moving."

"Your death, not mine," she said with a shrug, and headed for the house.

The meal was very cordial. McFee never once mentioned my staying down longer. I wonder if he knew how weak I felt. Still, it was time for me to go on. Nothing would be settled until Dingus and Seawell were behind bars. Why I felt so strong that their arrest was my responsibility, I wasn't certain. I kept remembering saving Seawell from his partner's wrath—I should have let them kill each other.

Kathreen packed some food for us to take. Stout thanked her for it and put the poke in her saddlebags.

McFee and I talked about the morning, how the rain cleared out the air, and how everything was so crystal clear.

"Don't ride to Texas in one day, lad," he warned. "But I know what's on your mind, and I hope you find those buggers. Here, take this bottle of whiskey. You may need the painkiller."

I accepted the bottle, he dismissed my offer to pay him, so I thanked him again. There was genuine concern written in his green eyes, but McFee was a man who knew what I had to do. Stout was already mounted when I stuck the bottle in my saddlebags.

I took the reins and then put my foot in the stirrup. The sharp lance in my chest took my breath away as I swung up, but I was seated and reined Baldy around.

"You be careful of them ribs," McFee said.

"I will. Thanks, Barney. Thanks, Kathreen."

She nodded. I knew she wanted to remind me about writing my cousin as she stood there smiling in her best blue dress. Her copper hair shone from many brushings, all prim and proper. If a man had been looking for him a fine hostess—Kathreen McFee would be an excellent choice for a wife. Myself, I much preferred the cowgirl nudging the black with her spurs.

Stout walked her horse leaving the ranch yard. I expected her to jog and for my ribs to complain. It would be a long day.

Midday we were in sight of a single store building. A set of weathered corrals and a windmill stood across the road from the false-fronted structure. This was Linter's, the main place of commerce in the North Cut.

"Sasperillia time." Stout winked and smiled at me. "That's one big treat we always take at Linter's."

"Looks like he's the only one in town."

"Most of us figured he'd leave here after his wife died, and then we wouldn't have a store. But Carl seems to have adjusted to the fact."

"She been dead long?" I asked.

"Two years, I guess. Myrtle was a happy little lady. Kinda like a mother to the three of us girls. She answered lots of questions that Paw couldn't."

"You were close to her?"

"She taught us how to dance too."

"She was a helluva good teacher."

I swear Stout blushed at my comment. She dismounted and I eased off the horse.

"Carl! Carl, where are you?" she called, going inside as I caught my short breath and let the chill of hurting subside standing beside Baldy. I studied the corral and windmill as the spells of pain subsided like water lapping on a lake shore.

"Locke, come here!" Stout shouted. "Carl's been hurt!"

I raced inside and saw Stout on her knees holding a man with blood on his face.

"Is he breathing?"

"Yes, but he's bleeding all over."

I felt for my pistol and straightened. Whoever did this couldn't be far away.

"Where are you going?" she shouted.

"I need to see if they're still around." My sore chest heaved to find air as I ran outside with my Colt in my hand. I paused to catch up on the porch. There was nothing but a sea of low purple sagebrush and some pinkish rock outcropping. Beyond that, junipers and piñons dotted the rolling country, but there was no sign of any riders. They couldn't have gone far. I needed to look for their tracks. There was always something distinctive about a horse's hoofprint. My grandfather could tell who passed by his farmhouse on the country road by pointing special prints out to me. He took a lot of pride when his grandson made out each distinct print in the dust.

I went back inside, wishing for more energy. It would be hard riding after them alone. Someone needed to stay and tend to storekeeper Linter.

He was sitting up when I returned.

"My, who's this?" he asked, "That ain't H.B."

"No, that's Locke McTavish, Carl," she said, moving around on her haunches beside him as the balding man sat propped against the counter. Stout had a flour sack towel for him to hold to his cut forehead. I joined the two of them, squatted carefully on my boot heels across from Stout. I was curious about who had hit him.

"Pistol-whipped me, the big one with the beard did."

"Was the other one a little man?" I asked.

"Yes."

"That's them—Seawell and Dingus. How long ago?" I asked.

"They stole my watch!" Carl said, looking down at his vest. "Oh, I'd say not over thirty minutes, but I was out. They must have robbed my cash drawer." Carl made a wry face at the prospect of the robbery.

"That probably was their purpose. I was just wondering how long ago they left."

"Locke, you can't go after them by yourself," Stout said with a frown.

"You take care of him," I said, using her shoulder to help steady the rise to my feet. "I'm going to take some short circles to look for their tracks and be back."

"What if you faint?"

"Then I'll just have to faint. Stout, I want these devils. They'll keep doing these vicious crimes until we stop them."

"They're tough," Linter warned me with a pained exhale.

I nodded that I'd heard his warning. I wished there was more I could do for his comfort, but she could do all that. I turned, adjusted the Colt, and started toward the door.

Silhouetted against the outside light, someone

stood in the doorway. Dressed in knee-high boots, red breechclout, blue shirt with some gold trim, and an unblocked hat on his head was a powerful-built Indian armed with a new repeating rifle. My heart stopped. An Apache! My fist closed on the hard rubber handle of the Colt. How many more were there?

CHAPTER
15

Don't shoot!" a young army officer shouted, and stepped in front of the Indian. "This man is a scout for the U.S. cavalry."

I turned to Stout for an answer as a tall slender man about my age in a blue uniform came down the aisle holding his hands out to halt my actions. Satisfied there was no threat, I let the Colt settle back down in my holster.

"That is my chief scout, Alkie Tie, which is the best I can say his name. My name is Lieutenant Gary Woods. What happened to *him?*" The officer looked shocked at Linter's condition.

"Nothing much, Lieutenant. I got my head in the way of some dang outlaw's pistol barrel earlier," Carl said, as Stout helped him to his feet.

"Ma'am, I'm sorry, I didn't realize there was a lady present," Woods said, sweeping off his hat with the gold braid hatband.

"That's all right, Lieutenant. This is Carl Linter, who owns the store. I'm Stout Rice, and he's Locke McTavish."

"Nice to meet all of you. May I examine the cut?" Woods asked. "I have some skills at suturing wounds."

"Sewing them," I said, to answer Stout's questioning look. She nodded that she understood.

"Has anyone seen any Apaches?" Woods asked carefully, scrutinizing the cut. "Yes, a dozen stitches should close that very well. Do you have a needle and fine catgut?"

"I'll get some," Stout offered.

"Those Indians attacked us three days ago," I said, holding up my bandaged left arm. "They stole some good horses too."

"A few weeks ago, they had a big war dance on the reservation and someone gave them a lot of bad whiskey. There were some fights, and eight bucks we know of, along with two or three squaws, left San Carlos. We've trailed them for a week."

"Will this do?" Stout asked the lieutenant, handing him the catgut and a hooked needle.

"Very good, ma'am. You live around here I suppose, Miss Rice?"

"Yes, my family has a ranch here in North Cut."

"Well, it certainly is my pleasure to meet you."

"Mine too," Stout said.

I was growing weary of Woods's flirtation with my girl. Let him get on with his sewing on Linter and find his own woman to talk to. Disgruntled with the situation, I headed for the front door and to look for the tracks of those outlaws.

A dozen Indians sat on their low-headed horses. They had been riding hard, I had little doubt, as I could see from the condition of their mounts. The chief scout rose from his seat on the porch stoop.

"You see Apaches?" Alkie Tie asked me.

"Yes. Three days ago they attacked Miss Rice and myself somewhere up north and west of here."

"You killed one of them," the head scout said. The other scouts heard Alkie Tie's words and nodded to affirm his statement. "We found where they buried him. But the others, they scatter like cottonwood seed."

"They have Miss Rice's palomino—big yellow horse. If you find it, I'll pay you forty bucks gold for its return."

Alkie Tie grinned and showed his even white teeth. "We find that horse."

"You know about tracks?" I figured those Indians could trail a titmouse to hell and back if they had found the place where I killed that Apache. I didn't think another human being could locate that place once we left it behind. I would have to write home something about that incident if it didn't sound too boastful.

He nodded.

"Two men just robbed this store. And they must have ridden away a short while ago."

Alkie Tie nodded and then spoke to the scouts in Apache. They turned their horses to scatter and look for tracks. I felt very smug at my use of Apache scouts to find Seawell and Dingus's trail.

In a moment a wizen-faced hatless scout rode back to where Alkie Tie and I waited. I realized at some time this man had been horribly burned, and taut lines in his cheeks were scars from that accident. He spoke to his boss and they came to a head, nodding agreement in Apache.

"Two go south." Alkie Tie pointed to the mountains. "You go to Globe and the mines that way. The trail is old and not clear. But Apaches used it long time ago to come here when they were free."

"Thanks," I said. I would need some jerky to eat, plus some cheese and crackers to put in my saddlebags. My chest was sore, but not so bad I couldn't travel. Every moment I sat around, those two were getting farther and farther away.

I went back inside. Lieutenant Woods was still doctoring Linter with Stout's assistance. I helped myself. I cut some cheese off the block on the counter, put some crackers in a poke. I didn't see any worms or weevils on them. The jerky was dark and in a large crock.

"Helped myself to some cheese, crackers, and jerky," I said to Carl as he winced under the lieutenant's needlework. "Left you four bits on the counter to cover it."

"Be fine!" Carl nearly stood up from the chair when Woods pulled his stitch tight. "Could you make them hurt a little more?"

"Maybe." Woods laughed, and then grinned privately at Stout, holding his next thread dipped in whiskey to disinfect it.

"We'll be through here in a moment," Stout said to me.

"Will Carl be all right by himself? You going to leave him?"

"He'll be fine," she said. "He's getting better every minute."

"Oh, I may die!" Carl shouted as Woods pulled another stitch through the wound. The man could sew. Woods was doing a very professional job, and I wished he'd been around to work on my arm. The scars on it would be wide and forever. I was just lucky I had the use of it after such a cut.

I opened and closed my right fist, becoming more aggravated at the officer for the attention he paid Stout. Quite frankly, I wasn't in the mood for any competition when it came to Stout Rice.

"You run along and be careful," Carl said to the two of us as we left him and the officer.

I thanked Alkie Tie, who was with his scouts, swigging down bottles of sarsaparilla on the front porch.

"Where you want yellow horse?" the scout asked.

"Bring it here! Carl will pay you, we'll get it later," I said as Stout and I prepared to mount.

"Does he know where Gold is?" she asked.

"No, but if he finds him, he'll bring him here for the reward."

"That was nice of you, thinking of that," she said as we turned our horses and headed south.

"I needed to make some points after that fancy army dude in there had you all in a twitter."

"A twitter?"

"You know what I mean. Woods was a slick-talking rascal."

"He seemed very nice to me."

"Nice?" I snorted in disbelief. I kicked Baldy into a lope. Those outlaws were getting away, and I didn't have time to talk about that damn glib-tongued lieutenant.

"You get any good directions from those scouts?" she asked, riding beside me.

"No, why?"

"I never took this trail south before," Stout said.

"If they went over it, so can we."

"I guess. You're the boss, McTavish."

I looked over at her in disbelief. I was the boss? Me, the pilgrim from Illinois?

"What's wrong?" she shouted over the drum of our horses running.

"Not a thing, Stout, not a thing."

The vast mountains we rode through held little vegetation except for giant beds of prickly pear, some scrub sagebrush, and a yucca plant she called the century plant because it only bloomed once in a hundred years, then it died.

"Apaches made beer from the roots of it," she explained as we walked our mounts.

"Wonder what it tasted like?" I asked, observing the almost barren mountainsides towering around us.

"Probably bad, but it was the only beer they had."

"You know, we'll more than likely have to sleep out under the stars tonight," I said, looking at the long shadow the range to the west cast on us.

"We may get to the Silver Creek community by dark," Stout said while riding beside me.

"Who lives there?"

"Mormons and a few ranchers."

"I thought you never—"

"I never was down there, but I know about it."

We rested our horses in the dying red and yellow

sundown as twilight swallowed the shadows. The irrigated green fields along the creek were fast fading into the darkness.

"You know anyone that lives down there?" I asked.

"No, but I'll bet we can buy a meal, grain our horses good, and sleep in a haystack."

I looked over at her and grinned. There were times being in the company of Stout Rice reminded me of being with another boy instead of a very eligible lady.

"We going to sit here all night or go on?" she asked impatiently.

I followed her down the slope.

We rode up to a small ranch house. A hatless small man in his fifties came out.

"Evening, folks. You and the missus light, we're fixing to eat," he said, as if he had been acquainted with us all our lives.

"We really can't impose on you, sir," I said.

"Impose, nothing. My name's Kincaid. You got something against beans?"

"No."

"Then you and that fine wife of yours tie up them broncs and come inside."

"Mr. Kincaid, this is Stout Rice. She isn't my wife. I'm Locke McTavish."

"She'd make a fine one. You're from those Rices I heard of up in North Cut?" he asked her.

"Yes, my father's Ewell Rice."

"I met him once. Come on inside." We followed him inside. "That's Lenore," he said, indicating the Mexican woman at the stove. "This here's Locke and Stout."

"We didn't mean to arrive at mealtime," I apolo-

gized to the rather handsome woman I guessed to be
in her thirties.

The woman dismissed my concern. "He always
brings home guests. There is plenty."

"Wash up over there and get a seat," Kincaid said
like a hen fussing over new chicks.

Seated at the large table, Stout talked to the woman,
who appeared very pleasant. Kincaid passed me the
bowl of red beans.

"You ranch up there?" he asked.

"I hope to," I said. "I just came to this country."

"I kinda figured that. I heard the names of most of
them ranchers up there, and I never had heard of you
before."

"Stout and I are after some outlaws that have been
killing and robbing folks the last two weeks. They may
have rode by here today."

"They didn't stop. They do that to your arm?" he
asked.

"No, some renegade Apaches did that a week ago."

"Apaches!" Lenore gasped, holding her throat.

"They weren't around here!" Kincaid said sharply
to reassure the woman.

"You saw them?" she asked, her brown eyes large as
saucers.

"Locke killed one of them in a fight," Stout said.

Lenore crossed herself twice mentioning Mary,
mother of god. The complexion of her face turned
pasty. Obviously, the mere mention of Apaches made
her fear-filled.

"The army scouts are looking for them. They'll find
'em," I said to reassure her.

"Lieutenant Woods and a dozen scouts were at Linter's store at noon today," Stout told the woman.

I wasn't sure all our assurances would salve Lenore's upset.

"Those Apaches preyed on the Mexican people for years," Kincaid explained.

"They killed many members in my family," Lenore said. "They are the devil's butchers."

"How many were there?" Kincaid asked.

"Alkie Tie, the chief scout, said originally eight men and some women left San Carlos. Four, maybe five, attacked us. One of those is dead and I think we wounded some more, but it happened so fast and all at night."

"You're lucky to be alive. Who are these killers you're looking for?"

"Serval Dingus and Mink Seawell."

Kincaid shook his head and I explained all of it from the start. I'd been in Arizona little over a week, killed an Apache Indian, had a very sore cut-up arm, broken ribs, and had several altercations with two outlaws. What had Stout told me? I'd better wear a big gun because fists would not resolve all the problems in this land.

We thanked and left Lenore and Kincaid before dawn. According to our host, it was forty miles over some rough mountains to Globe. There was a wagon road to Globe but not a great one, according to Kincaid. However, the folks along Silver Creek brought in most of their goods from Globe by that route. That separated them more from the North Cut people, who went the other way, to the railhead at Flagstaff for their items.

The sun was a lot hotter in this desert region we were descending into. My ribs hurt worse that morning than the first one. I tried to hide the fact from Stout as we rode south. Her disapproval of whiskey-drinking forced me to grit my teeth and go on despite the pain.

"You going to hurt till you fall off that dang horse before you start on the whiskey?" she finally asked.

"Thinking about it," I said.

"I figured you'd pass out first," she said, and rode in close, unbuckled the saddlebags, and jerked out the bottle. "You better have some of this."

I agreed and accepted the bottle from her. The hurting was bad enough to need something. I wondered, as I drank from the neck of the bottle, where those two uncouth criminals were hiding. I'd be glad when our outlaw-chasing days were over and my sides quit paining me.

CHAPTER
16

Globe looked busy. A mixture of houses and tents, and adobe, wood, and packing-crate construction lined the canyons that served as the streets. On the hills, the smelters belched yellow, sick-looking smoke into the air. On the sidewalks, men frosted in miner's dust looked hard as Stout and I rode down the crowded, narrow twisted avenue. I hoped to recognize Dingus and Seawell's horses at the hitch rail in front of some saloon. Drays, double freight wagons, teams of oxen, mules—even pack trains—jammed the street and forced us to detour around them.

At the first wagon yard, I dismounted with a hard catch in my side. A tall man with gray sideburns came out of the small office and gave me the once-over, as if I didn't belong there.

"Yes?" he asked.

"I'm looking for two men rode in here the last few

days. One's tall with a black beard. The other's small, looks like a weasel," I told the liveryman, who kept a skeptical eye on two of us.

He glanced over at Stout as she sat the black and held Baldy's reins for me. "Must be five hundred men answer that description around town, mister. You ain't from these parts, are you?"

I shook my head, trying to suppress my growing anger at the man's outward insolence toward me. Maybe the whiskey I'd drunk for the pain made me so quick to anger. I didn't consider myself drunk, but he was edging me into taking action.

"See, you got a lot to learn in this country. Take my advice, a man out here that minds his own business— he'll live longer."

"These men killed a pal of mine," I said, considering Badger would have been my friend if he'd lived.

"You still ain't qualified to go looking for no hard cases. Ride up to Marshal Two Lines's office up the street and ask him to handle this matter. You got a warrant for them anyway?"

"Yes," I said, taking the reins from Stout. "It's called the Constitution of the United States, the Bill of Rights, and this damn Colt on my hip. Thanks for being no damn help at all!" I swung on the horse and jerked him around. That liveryman had his nerve telling me I had no authority.

"You'll wish you'd listened to my advice," he said after us.

"You're as all-fired mad as I can ever remember seeing you," Stout said under her breath, moving in close as we left the surly man and rode up the crowded street.

"We've ridden good horses into the ground looking for those two. Where did he get his gall coming off like that?"

"Figure he'd save you getting killed maybe?"

I looked at her hard. "I can take care of myself."

"Damn, I believe you can," she said, and idly swung the ends of the reins in a circle.

"Wait here," I said, and dismounted again. I handed her the reins and headed for the green-louvered batwing doors of McCoy's Saloon. I was always told, in the right bar for a price you could hire the devil to fire the furnaces of hell and cause a great thaw in the dead of winter. Someone with the name of McCoy, a fellow Scot, too, would at least be civilized to another kinsman.

"What'll it be?" a barkeep asked, wiping the polished bar top with a white rag.

"I'm new here and need some information," I told the man.

"Whiskey is two bits a jigger, and beer's a dime a glass. Information is free."

"Good, McTavish is my name. I just rode in, and I'm unfamiliar with the lay of the town. Two killers rode in here the past days, and I want to know their whereabouts."

"Who are they?"

"Serval Dingus and Mink Seawell."

"Never heard of them, but they're probably down in Mexican town. Most wanted kind stay out of sight in those cantinas down there. What hotel will you be staying at?"

"Which one is respectable enough for a lady?" I asked.

"The Grand."

"Good, I'll be at the Grand. I'll pay for this information about Seawell and Dingus."

"It'll cost you ten dollars for me to send my man to go look for them, and if they're in Globe, you'll know before"—the man turned and looked at the clock on the shelf—"ten this evening."

"Give me a shot of that whiskey." I put a ten-dollar gold piece and a quarter on the bar. Finally I was getting some place. "What was the name?"

"Lester McCoy." He slapped a shot glass on the bar, filled it to the lip with a flurry and never spilled a drop.

I raised the small glass, toasted Lester McCoy, and tossed it down. Whew, McFee did make much better whiskey, but I never coughed on the bar brand. I left the saloon and rejoined Stout.

"What now?" she asked.

"We put our horses in a livery and get a hotel room. Take a bath even, and wait for the word from my man."

"What word?" she asked, looking skeptical at me.

"If those two are here, we'll know where they're at before midnight."

"Oh, you're in charge. I forgot." Stout smiled at me.

From the third floor of the Grand, I looked out the window at the busy street. We both were registered in one room as Mr. and Mrs.—a large sign over the desk said No Single Females Admitted to Hotel. Stout did not seem upset about the matter. My intentions were honest regarding her.

Stout, at the moment, was behind the Chinese folding screen splashing in the tin tub.

"I'm sorry we had to register like that," I tried to apologize.

"I saw that sign, nothing else you could do. What did all this hotel business set you back?"

"It was cheaper than I thought."

"How much was that?"

"Two dollars a night and fifty cents for the bath."

"We could have stayed out in the hills for free."

"I know that, but we'll know if and where those two are located in a few hours."

"Are you going to use this Marshal Two-something?"

"Maybe."

"Maybe?" she asked, obviously standing up, for I heard the rush of water.

"Do you think I should?" I asked.

"Yes, then we'll have the marshal hold them for the sheriff in Flagstaff. He should have received word on all the problems they've caused by now."

"What about your U.S. marshal friend?"

"We can wire him in Prescott, I guess. I do feel cleaner. Thanks. This is much nicer than the hills."

"Good, we'll go to the restaurant downstairs for supper after a while."

"Have they got some cowboy diner down the street somewhere? I don't like to eat in a hotel restaurant."

"Tonight we'll eat in one. How's that?" Stout would have to get used to a little luxury once in a while.

"Makes me itchy all over," she said from behind the screen.

"Don't worry, we're nearly through with this part of our lives."

"Everyday living is going to be halfway hard to go

back to on the ranch after all this, isn't it?" She came out straightening her blouse and smoothing down her full skirt.

"Not for me. You'll certainly look fine to go out dining anywhere."

"It ain't the outside fine part that bothers me, it's the girl inside these duds that is worried."

Supper in the hotel salon was uneventful. Stout looked as proper as any woman in the place to me. There were a few younger women I recognized as companions to some of the older men with diamond stickpins in their ties. We feasted on their special, roasted pig, potatoes, sliced white bread, and fresh green beans. The waiter commented several times how the beans were picked daily from local fields.

The food was good. My ribs hurt from riding all day and I felt uncomfortable, but I'd expected it. Stout had enough charm and grace to make me very proud. I thought she was the most attractive woman in the place. After supper we took a short stroll in the growing darkness around the hotel block and the more respectable businesses to let the daytime heat escape our room, then we returned upstairs. I was anxious to learn if my scheme had worked.

There was a rap on the door, and I bolted out of the chair. It was now dark outside, so I had no idea what time it was.

"Yes?" I asked cautiously.

"Señor McTavish?"

I opened the door and greeted a short Mexican with white clothing and sandals. He stood with his great sombrero over his heart.

"Lester, he sent me to tell you that those men you

want are in the Estra Cantina. They were pretty drunk a while ago."

"Who are you?" I asked. "Can you show me this place?"

"*Sí.* My names is Victor Juarez. I can take you there."

I looked at Stout. I wanted her to stay in the room.

"Let's go," she said, and I was forced to agree. I slipped on the long duster and my hat and nodded to Stout as she finished doing the same. She did not approve of my actions—I could see that in her eyes—she wanted me to go secure the marshal. But she never broached the subject. Then we left with Victor.

The streets in the Mexican part of Globe were narrow and noisy. In the distance someone was singing and strumming a guitar. A train of burros loaded with firewood threaded their way through the streets and forced us to detour around them. I felt for the Colt and straightened it under my long coat when Victor stopped.

"There is the Estra Cantina," he said, pointing down the hill to a bar. "They were at a table in the back when my friend showed them to me."

"Will anyone come to their aid if I arrest them in there?" I studied the adobe building. The three of us stood in the shadows. Light flooded into the dark street from the doorway and the single front window.

"No, they're bad-mouthed gringos and pistoleros. No one in there would care if you killed them."

"I don't think it's a good idea—" Stout whirled at the gunfire.

Shots erupted in the night from inside the saloon. I

looked hard at Juarez as I moved her behind us with my arm. He shrugged his small shoulders under his poncho without a word. The shrill screams of women and angry men's voices filled the night as the cantina lights went out. Horses shied at the hitch rail.

Dark figures ran outside, but I could not make them out as I cautiously hurried forward. Their guns flashed flames of red as they shot back inside the saloon entrance. My gun drawn, I rushed around a great ox cart, but I still couldn't see enough of the faces of the shooters in the darkness. I had to be sure. Even if I could shoot them without hitting someone else, I had to be absolutely certain it was them. My eyes strained to make them out.

Then they were on their horses, cursing and riding west. Somehow, I knew the men I sought had just left more blood on the cantina floor. Stout was beside me holding her revolver.

"Was that them?" she asked.

"I think so." I shook my head in disappointment, still concentrating on the cantina.

Victor spoke in Spanish to someone who rushed outside of the bar into the street with a pistol in his hand. We stood in the street as the sounds of their horses grew more faint, the two men speaking loudly in their native tongue.

"Señor," Victor turned to me. "Those gringos you seek just shot this man's brother in there, and that was them rode away."

"Why did they shoot him?" I asked.

" 'Cause they didn't like his smile, they said."

I nodded that I understood. Sewell and Dingus were insane murderers when they were drunk. Crestfallen with the fact of their escape, I holstered the Colt and then paid the apologetic Victor two dollars for his troubles. We'd pick up their trail in the morning. I turned to face Stout. I should never have let her come along; it was too dangerous. Maybe I should have done things differently. No, my scheme hadn't worked was all. Dangerous or not, I would have to include her. She would never stand for being left behind.

I stepped back in the shadows. There wasn't much for either of us to say. We drifted toward the hotel, past the generous propositions of the lovely Latin doves and the offers to win big at gambling wheels promised by the barkers on the sidewalk. Finally, out of breath, I paused before we entered the lobby of the Grand Hotel.

"You all right?"

"Fine, just thoroughly disappointed they got away." Stout agreed with me.

From some reserves I gathered the last remainder of my strength and climbed the staircase to the third floor.

"Well?" she asked when she let me inside our room.

"I couldn't be certain in all the confusion, so I never shot. Was that wrong?"

"You did the right thing." She closed the door and pressed her back to it. "The whole time I worried about us going down there alone."

I smiled at her to dismiss her concern. I wanted to kiss her bad enough, but that would seem cheap under the circumstances of this room that we shared as a lie.

"You get the bed," I said, and took off my coat and holster.

"No, you're the sore one, you take the bed."

"I'm sleeping on the floor."

"Locke McTavish, get on that bed!" she ordered.

I was tired enough not to argue any more. "This isn't how I want it!"

She never answered me and busied herself spreading our bedrolls on the floor. I sprawled on top of the bed, tired and pained. Next thing I felt was Stout gently removing my boots. I'd never have been able to bend over and get them off in my state.

"Stout?"

"Yes."

"I was glad you were there tonight. I won't ever leave you behind. I promised myself that tonight. We're partners."

"And we'll find them," she said softly to reassure me. I agreed, and fell asleep.

CHAPTER
17

The stagecoach to Florence Junction was ready to leave. Our horses were boarded at the livery; we'd rent more if necessary. I held Stout's hand for balance as she climbed into the coach. The best information I could gain early that morning was that the first place west of Globe the pair might show up was the stage stop at Florence Junction. If Seawell and Dingus rode that far, the main road split there, and they'd either go south toward Tucson or west to Phoenix—according to the people I talked with earlier.

The stage ride suited Stout, and she mentioned the coach might be easier on my sore ribs. While waiting on the boardwalk in front of Skyler's Stage and Express Lines office, we learned we would share the compartment with a small man wearing glasses. From past experience I knew they'd allow the lady the choice of seats. The best place to ride was facing the rear, so I told Stout to take the front bench for us.

Four Eyes took the bench in the rear. He looked like a man who'd ruined his vision in a poorly lighted office going over columns of numbers. His pasted-on smile reminded me of a tomcat who had eaten a rotten dead fish, pleased with the meal but not sure how it would settle in his stomach. I figured he would become road sick before we made the Junction. I recalled some previous unpleasant trips with such a passenger.

The driver left Globe with a hardy "Hi-Ho" and the crack of a whip that jerked the three teams of horses to alertness. They surged into their collars. From his perch above us the driver shouted directions to a variety of female names. Actually, he called out the names of various horses when they failed to meet his expectations. Stage drivers weren't suppose to swear when carrying female passengers, so I knew our driver was having vocabulary problems on the high seat with Stout tucked in the leather bench beside me.

"They've got a shotgun guard up there," the little man said. "Been a passel of robberies of the gold boxes on this line."

"That's why they've got a guard?" I asked.

"Sure. Why, they been robbing this stage line more than any other because it always carries the biggest boxes of gold."

I didn't understand why Skyler's boxes were so much bigger. "What do you mean?"

"The man owns this line is brother-in-law to the mine superintendent. You get it now?" He cackled like a little hen, so proud of his knowledge.

"They've got a special big shipment today," the man said, looking expectantly out the side window at the passing head-high desert brush he called grease-wood.

"What's your business in Globe?" I asked.

"Oh, I don't have one right now."

Stout looked at me with a question on her face. I had no answer for her. I didn't know what he did for a living. My ribs did ride better in the coach than on horseback, but it was not superior to a railroad car for comfort.

"You know, there's going to be a robbery today?" the man said and chuckled.

"I've been studying on it," I said, "since you told us about all the gold up there."

He drew a small pistol from a shoulder holster, .22 caliber, I estimated. "Don't you two do anything foolish." he warned. "You'll be hearing shots any minute. One move—"

My swift boot toe send the gun flying from his hand, and I lurched on the little man, grasping his lapels in my hands. I wanted to shake his small yellow teeth out of his head. Stout had his empty gun hand in her hands and was beating it on the door facing.

"Warn the driver," I told Stout.

She let go and looked at the man in disgust. "They're going to rob you any minute!" she yelled out the window.

"How you know, lady?" the guard asked.

"This little weasel back here told us, and my husband has him. You stay alert. It's going to happen in a few minutes."

"Thanks," he said, and the driver shouted to the horses to go faster.

"Now, what's your name?" I demanded, hauling

the man up to my face. The fact he had drawn a gun on Stout and me made me mad, and I was ready to pitch him out of the stage.

"Carter, Emil Carter. Listen, you'll be sorry when the gang gets here."

"The only sorry one will be you. How many are there in the gang?"

"Twenty!"

"Quit lying to me and tell me the truth!" I shook him like a rag doll to get the right answer.

"Four, counting the kid holds the horses!"

"There will only be three holdup men," Stout shouted to the guard.

"Good. You folks stay down," the guard hollered.

"Heck, no, we're going to shoot at them too," Stout said.

"You're certainly welcome to shoot all you want, ma'am, all you want. I was worried for your safety!"

"Thanks," Stout yelled, and settled back on the seat. "They're in for a big surprise, aren't they, Locke?"

"They sure will be if he was supposed to hold the passengers hostage. Give me your kerchief, I need to tie him up," I said. I quickly trussed Carter's hands behind his back with Stout's neckerchief and left him facedown on the backseat. When I sat down beside Stout, he began kicking and threatening me. I became so furious at him, I rose and gagged him with my neckerchief.

"That ought to shut him up," I said.

Stout grinned. "He's certainly a half-size outlaw. Did he think that peashooter would hold us in check? Wonder what the rest of them are like."

"Don't underestimate him, he's probably been the one who gave the robbers all their information about past shipments."

Stout agreed. She took another look at the little man in his checkered coat, bound and gagged and on his belly in the rear seat. I watched her shake her head, still in disbelief.

"Here's something to shoot them with." The guard handed down a Winchester for us to use. "Give it to your husband."

I took the long gun and drew it inside the coach window. Kneeling on the floor, I levered in a shell as we rocked back and forth.

"Your husband?" I asked, and glanced toward her.

Stout had a wistful look of mischief on her face. "Well, it does sound more respectful among strangers."

"Fine with me."

Gunshots cut the air above the rush of the coach and horses. The driver shouted to the teams to go. I leaned out the window to take a waving bead at one of the masked robbers alongside the road ahead. My bullet took his horse. Both horse and rider went down in a pile.

The guard's shotgun barrel answered them in two separate thunderous blasts. We swept by the would-be highwaymen with a deadly spray of Colt and rifle fire from Stout, the guard on top, and me. The would-be robbers headed for cover as we swept away.

Flush-faced and with traces of black powder ash on her cheeks, Stout looked about to bust as she settled back on the seat. The driver urged the horses away from the highwaymen. She looked very beautiful holding her pistol, a trace of blue smoke wafting from the muzzle. I squatted on the floor beside the door and looked at her in amazement.

"You folks all right?" the guard shouted down as we raced westward.

"Fine," I said, staring deep into her blue eyes.

"You recognize any of them?" the guard asked.

"No, but this little rat we have tied up down here will tell us all their names," I said.

"Yeah, we'll get that from him. Good job. You'll get a reward too!" the guard shouted.

We didn't answer him. I rose from my knees, and Stout held her arms out to help me. I could not resist one moment longer. We began kissing. Strange thing, we began hugging each other like we'd never known the other one was so sweet or nice to hold. My ribs hurt, but not bad enough to quit.

Florence Junction proved to be a smattering of adobe buildings inside a compound, A fortlike wall around it had been built to ward off the threat of Apaches who once sulked in the nearby purple mountains, called Peraltas, that provided a backdrop for the stage stop.

"You can get food and coffee inside," the driver announced, opening the coach door for us. "Where is that little vermin that intended to help those highwaymen?" He shoved a Winchester barrel inside and poked Carter in the face with the barrel. The man's eyes were wide with fear as he moaned under my gag.

"We couldn't stand the noise he made," I said to explain the gag as I helped Stout down.

"He better make lots of noise about who those

robbers were and what his role was in this robbery business. I'd have already fed him to the damn buzzards," the driver said, "but I wanted the names of those other robbers." He jerked the man out of the coach.

A big man in a white shirt joined them, and they shook the little man for the answers. I headed Stout for the main building after a quick check around. They looked very capable of handling Carter.

A Mexican woman waited on us. She brought coffee in thick mugs along with beans, snowy tortillas, and cooked tomatoes in bowls.

"Do you understand English?" I asked, not seeing anyone else to speak to since all the men were changing horses or occupied with Carter out front.

The woman nodded her head. "Oh, *sí señor*."

"Did two men ride by here since last night? One was tall with a beard, one was small."

She shook her head. "I've not seen them."

"Maybe they haven't ridden this far," Stout said, holding her coffee mug and blowing on the steaming liquid.

"It's past noon now. I can't believe they went the other way."

"Maybe they rode to Florence and did not stop here," the woman said.

"There's your answer," Stout said.

"No, they had no reason *not* to stop here. No one here knew them, and the word was not out yet on the Globe shooting. Not that quickly."

"What do you think?" Stout asked.

"I want to wait here for the next stage and see if

they come by. I have a hunch that they're still coming on jaded horses."

"Whatever. Do you have rooms here?" Stout asked the woman.

"Two rooms to rent us," I said to correct her.

"Oh, yes, you can stay here. The rooms are by the wall. They are very clean, *señora.*"

"Good, we want two."

"Sí, señor, I will have someone make the beds for you while you eat," she said, not questioning our needs.

The driver came inside. He crossed the room to join us. He set his hat aside and sat down at the plate the woman had set for him.

"You're really quick-thinking, mister. You two sure saved us from another robbery." The driver shook his head as he studied the food. "You know, that dang Carter has been their spy in Globe since last winter. The stage lines and express company will pay you two hundred dollars reward for your part in this deal."

"Send the reward to Locke McTavish, Double R Ranch, Flagstaff," Stout said.

The driver fished out a piece of paper from his shirt and stub of a pencil to write down the address.

"What's your business anyway, McTavish?" he asked.

"Ranching someday, I hope."

The man nodded; he believed me. I looked at Stout holding the coffee cup in her hands, her elbows on the tabletop, as was her habit. Even she slowly nodded in approval. Confident in my newly won status, I dished out some more beans on a fresh tortilla and wrapped up another Mexican sandwich.

"Oh, we'll be staying here tonight," I explained between bites.

"Honeymooning, huh?" he asked. "I kinda seen that. Well, good luck to you two. Sorrel Davis is that big man out there. He's putting Carter in his jail. Sorrel runs this station. He'll show you and the missus a good stay."

I wasn't certain if Stout was going to blush away or burst out laughing. She had to turn her head. The driver didn't seem to notice her. The big burly shotgun guard came in dragging his scattergun. He nodded a hello and sat down to eat.

"The honeymooners ain't going on with us," the driver told him.

"Lord, I'd never have left the Grand Hotel." The guard laughed aloud. "But we're sure grateful you two were in that coach, or Cyrus and I might be feeding buzzards back there ourselves. And, ma'am, I really appreciate how you can use a gun too. I saw your shooting."

Stout nodded that she heard him and brushed at her left eye.

"You all right?" I asked as she rose.

"Fine, I'll be back," she said, and left the room.

"You're a lucky man," the driver said, mopping out his plate with a tortilla, "that gal will do to ride out the storms with."

I agreed, thanked them, and went to see what was wrong with Stout. From the doorway I could see the activity in the stage stop yard. Half-naked Mexican children screamed and raced about the place. Three and four at a time, they used a still burro for a slide, swing, and even squatted under his belly for the shade.

"You the man captured that pint-size stage robber?"

"I'm Locke McTavish. You must be Sorrel Davis," I said, and shook his massive hand. "This is your fort?"

"Yes. I built it and been here forever. Fifteen years ago this was a tough place to build a stage stop. Apaches didn't like anyone close to their mountains of the gods. But I shot the damn horse out from under a little dried-up prune of an Apache chief by the name of Chacko something with my old buffalo gun at a half mile. They withdrew and we finished building these walls."

"I didn't quite do that well," I said, and showed him my bandaged arm and told him the story of the Apaches.

"You're a lucky man, McTavish. Apaches choose when they want to fight and usually do it when they can win. They ain't like the Cheyennes and the Sioux or even those Comanches—them Plains Indians fought for honor. Apaches only tangles with you to steal your horses or to take what you had or else to kill an enemy."

"Yes, I sure would like to get my . . . um . . . wife's good yellow horse back that they stole."

"Not much chance of that. Guess they told you Apaches eat horses when they're through with them. Excuse me, the stage is leaving. I need to tell the driver I'll hold Carter for the sheriff."

I watched the big man cross the yard. Stout joined me.

"He's the owner, Sorrel Davis." I explained to her. "He killed buffalo on the plains, fought Indians for this place."

"Folks in North Cut fought those same Indians. But we may be the last folks ever attacked by Indians around here." I noticed she was holding my arm. We wandered back for her to show me the small, neat rooms that the woman Dolores had prepared for us.

"They're nice," I agreed, looking in the small cubicles with the whitewashed walls and the wooden poster beds covered with clean quilts. I was more impressed with the fact that she held my arm.

"Want to see if anyone is coming?" Stout asked, motioning to the turret on top of the wall.

"Sure. We might see those two coming down the road."

We climbed the ladder and looked out the watchtower at the tall desert cactus with long arms like huge people waving at each other. I studied the road to the east. There was no sign of anyone coming. Where had those two gone? Had they doubled back to the North Cut country? I certainly hoped not.

"Well, everyone has written us together, haven't they?" Stout asked, peering out into the thick desert with the pale green weeping palo verde and lacy mesquite trees beneath the saguaros.

"Been a helluva courtship so far," I said, wanting to laugh about the past ten days together on the road and on the trail of the criminals.

"When you came to Arizona, what did you expect?" she asked.

"I was going to go ranching," I said. Stout chuckled. "What's so damn funny?" I demanded.

"Nothing, Locke McTavish, but two weeks ago you were as far away from being a rancher as anything I ever saw."

"Two weeks ago, huh? Would you mind so much today if I told those store clerks at Babbett Brothers store we were engaged?"

She shrugged and grew quiet. "It ain't really so."

"It could be, couldn't it?"

"Maybe."

"Would your sisters be all mad if you came home married to me?"

"If I what?" Stout blinked at me.

"You heard me."

"You've never asked me."

"Will you marry me, Stout Rice?"

She bobbed her head, yes.

I took her in my arms and we kissed deeply. Hearing Sorrel's voice in the courtyard, I hesitantly broke away from our embrace.

"Sorrel?" I shouted down at the big man as he crossed the yard on some mission. "Where is the nearest preacher or judge that can marry us?"

"In Florence." He pointed to the south. "Sixteen or so miles that way. "Hey I thought you already were—"

"We will be," I corrected him. "You have a buggy or rig we can rent to go there?"

He shaded his eyes looking up with a grin. "It'll be hitched in a few minutes for you two."

"You sure this is what you want to do?" Stout asked.

I was already started down the ladder. "Why, Stout

Rice, I knew I wanted to do this two weeks ago in Flagstaff. I'm more convinced now." I paused in the tower's trapdoor exit half out of the tower. "Next trip, will you tell those store clerks that you're my wife?"

"Sure."

CHAPTER
18

The wind was in our faces, and I let Sorrel's big bays have the bits. The light buggy slid all four narrow-rimmed wheels around the sandy corners on the Florence road. We headed down the straightaway across the desert of saguaros and prickly pear cactus leaving a great curtain of dust in our wake.

I stood up to see ahead, and Stout hugged my waist so I didn't fall out of the racing rig. I wanted to see the line of the Gila River ahead because Sorrel said there would be a ferry to pick us up. The river lay north of Florence, and I knew that meant we'd be close to finding someone to bless our union and make it—as my Aunt Jessica would say—respectable.

What would my family think of the marriage? I had not even given the matter a thought since becoming the prodigal one and leaving home. I never expected to find a wife before I had a ranch. Things worked out backwards.

"This is so wild," Stout said, shaking her head as if she didn't believe we were going through with it. "I don't have a wedding dress, flowers, or a ring even."

I shouted to the horses to hurry. We rounded another curve and I leaned against her. "I've got a ring if it'll fit you. Belonged to my grandmother. I've been saving it for this day. If it doesn't, we'll make it work somehow."

"Hee hah!" she cried at the horses to make them go faster. With one arm around my shoulders, Stout's other hand held the iron rail on the dashboard so she didn't fall out. Go horses, go! We're hurrying to find someone to sanction this union!

The road dropped down a grade, and I spotted the green line of the river.

"Florence," I said, and set back sawing the horses down to a trot. They blew and pranced in their confined pace as we drove up to the ferry landing.

The rope-held ferry came across the river for us as the sun sank in the west. I paced beside the buggy.

"You're sure this is what you want to do?" she asked.

I looked at her open-eyed, shocked that she would even ask. "Yes, I'm certain."

"You know, you can still back out?"

"Stout Rice, I'm not a quitter. I want to marry you. What about you? Your family isn't here. You don't have a lace gown."

"Guess I'd feel silly in a lace gown anyway." She shook her head and climbed off the seat. "We don't have a house or even a—guess we could use the line shack for a while."

"It'll work. That ferry sure is slow getting over here to pick us up."

"Or you're awfully impatient."

"Probably both."

The muddy Gila River swirled by as I watched and waited with my bride-to-be for the barge to finally cross to our side.

The horses loaded easily, obviously familiar with the hollow-sounding deck. Still, they were acting frisky, and I didn't want to risk them plunging over the side. Stout and I each held a horse by the bridle so that if they did act up, we could control them.

After the crossing, we unloaded and I paid the operator his fee. I helped Stout up, then I climbed on the seat and set out down the main street. One half block away, I saw the Catholic church with the plastered walls looking very serene. I reined the team to a halt.

"Would this do?" I asked.

"Certainly." Stout shrugged and took my hand to dismount.

I wondered if they'd marry non-Catholics. We'd ask them—all they could say was no. We undid our guns and put the holsters under the seat. After a long look into each other's face, we headed for the church's heavy wooden front doors, hand in hand.

Inside, the church's altar was lighted with flickering candles. Jesus was nailed on the cross high on the wall. We stood in the rear, wondering how to summon someone.

"Have you come to seek the Lord?" the priest asked. Wearing long robes, he came up the church aisle to greet us. He knew by the manner we had entered that we were lost and non-Catholics.

"We aren't Catholic," I said, and Stout agreed. "But we did want to get married in your church. This is a very nice one, sir." I looked at the high stained glass windows and the paintings of Christ and his struggles en route to the cross that lined the side wall.

"You would need instructions in the faith and a posting of your vows. All this takes time, my children."

"Time is what we don't have, sir. We just wanted to be married, blessed if we could be, and on our way."

He nodded as if he was deep in thought on the issue. "I could not marry you in the church, of course. That's out of the question."

"I understand you have rules, but I wondered— could you do it outside, maybe in a garden?" I asked. "Jesus did lots of things in the garden, didn't he?"

"Oh, you've read of him?"

"Yes, some. That's why we're here."

"Yes, I think that could be arranged. I will go get my book and some witnesses for such a joining. In these modern days no one has enough time for anything. Far be it for me to deny you two living in wedded matrimony. Kneel here and please pray for the things ahead in your life." He made the sign of the cross and left us alone.

We knelt as he said, and I found Stout's hand to squeeze.

"What will we pray for?" she asked quietly.

"Our life together forever."

Stout nodded and we both prayed hard as I can

remember to the image on the cross with Mary nearby in her blue dress. I knew Christ's mother was an image the Catholics held high. I also prayed all my Baptist relations forgave me, but their church wasn't on this block.

The priest returned, introduced himself as Father Nabors, and I gave him our names. He repeated them several times. Father Nabors then led us from the church into the garden. Two nuns came along, their hands in their sleeves, the gentle rising night wind tossing their white hoods. Father Nabors lit a few candle lamps because the sun was nearly down beyond the far-off mountains. I felt very somber as he began to read the wedding vows and we agreed with I dos.

"Do you have a ring?" the father asked.

"Yes, sir." I removed the velvet-wrapped ring from my coin purse. The cloth clung to the band, for it had been deep in my pocket for many years. I finally managed to free it. Father Nabors placed the gold circle on a pillow and blessed it, then he returned it to me and told me to place it on Stout's finger. It fit. Stout exhaled in relief and smiled warmly.

"I now pronounce you man and wife," he ended, and made another sign of the cross. Then he sprinkled a spray of water on us for some reason.

"Thank you," I said, a little awed by all the implications of the evening.

"You may kiss the bride," he said, and I did. Even the nuns smiled, and I thought they weren't supposed to do that.

"I must sign the wedding certificate," Father Nabors said, "and I will file it."

"Do you need money for all this," I said.

"Yes."

"Ten dollars?"

"That is too generous."

"It will be all right," I said, grateful the ceremony was over and feeling that my stomach was alive with worms.

"Where do I send the certificate?" he asked.

Stout gave him the ranch address. We thanked the nuns, who hugged both of us in genuine goodwill. We hurried hand in hand out of the courtyard. Our boot heels clattered on the rock walkway as we rushed for our conveyance, Stout's hand tight in mine.

The church's long shadows were cast on the waiting horses. I stopped and shielded her at my discovery. Two men were riding by in the street. It was them, Dingus and Seawell. Our guns were in the buggy box, and that was fifty feet from where we stopped.

"Look, that's the damn pilgrim!" Mink shouted. "Dingus, it's that tall guy beat you up in Flag."

"I see him!"

I spun Stout on her heel and herded her around the corner of the church building. I would have paid a fortune for a gun to use on them. Their pistol shots fractured the quiet night air and showered plaster down on Stout and me as we held to the wall of the sanctuary.

"Get out of here. This shooting sure will bring the damn law on us!" Mink shouted.

"Hell with the law. I want that sumabitch and her dead." Two more of his bullets slapped the stucco on the church.

"I'll get you!" Dingus swore and then, unable to

hold his rearing horse, bolted after his partner in a clatter of hooves.

I crossed the churchyard in long bounds, reached the wagon, and freed the Colt. By the time I was ready to shoot, they were already over half a block away. Shooting at them would be of no avail, and I might harm an innocent bystander. Damn. I let the gun barrel drop.

Stout was beside me wrestling her own gun out.

"What now?" she asked, out of breath.

"We better go find the law and let them handle it. Let's get in the wagon."

Marshal Hendricks was a tall man with a spare mustache. He had a way of looking very hard at everyone he conversed with, as if he distrusted them. At the moment that included a man and his bride who'd driven up to his office in a rig with high-headed horses and a wild story about two killers and prison escapees shooting at them in front of the Catholic church.

"Somewhere I might have the poster on those two," he said, drumming his desk with a pencil. "Seawell and Dingus, huh?"

"Yes, they shot at us not five minutes ago in front of the Catholic church," I said, almost put out with the man's lack of enthusiasm.

"And you've trailed them clear from North Cut, huh?"

"Yes, they even killed a man last night in Globe."

"They're tough *hombres,* huh?"

"They're in your town," I said. "We came in here to tell you this because you're the law."

"That's right. I'll handle them. You two don't need to worry about them ever again."

"We hope you can do that, Marshal Hendricks," Stout said, and rose to her feet, ready to leave him.

"Where will you two be so I can tell you when I got them locked up."

"Florence Junction. We'll be there a few days, I figure, before we head back home," I said, standing up and sharing a questioning look at my bride. Stout agreed with a nod.

"Those birds are as good as in my jail now." Hendricks kept drumming his desktop with the pencil and never offered to show us out.

On the sidewalk in front of his office, I searched all around in the inky night for any sign of the killers before I helped Stout up on the seat. She undid the reins, and once I was seated, she handed the lines to me.

"What do you think?" she asked under her breath, then nudged me in the side.

Hendricks had come out of the office with a sawed-off shotgun. He barely nodded to us as he started down the dark sidewalk. The only lighting up or down the night-shrouded street spilled out in patches from windows and doorways.

"Do you think that marshal'll get them?" Stout asked in a whisper.

"No, but he wouldn't listen."

"Locke, I know you won't be satisfied until those two are in jail."

"We've done all we can here for tonight, Mrs. McTavish. Let's go back."

Stout hugged my arm. "I'm ready."

I clucked to the horses and made a U-shaped turn in the dark street. I patted her hand to reassure her despite the crawly feeling up the skin on the back of my neck. We hadn't seen the last of those two vermin.

CHAPTER

19

A dull lantern with a smoked-up glass flickered on the porch of the ferry office. I tied off the reins and helped Stout down.

The night sky was sprayed with stars. They glistened on the dark Gila River rushing by. I knocked on the door, and a lanky thin man came from the desk with a put-out look on his face.

"Can we get a ferry ride across?" I asked the man as he scratched his sideburns and bent over to look at me, having to lower his head to see beneath the door casing. The man was tall, and the front door was short.

"I guess. Didn't you just come across?"

"A while ago. We just got married. Came over here to find a preacher."

"By Jove, that's nice," the man said, and stepped outside on the porch. He nodded to Stout as if he approved. "I wouldn't want to hold up no honey-mooners, would I?"

Stout looked at the stars like she wished I'd never told a soul about the event. My wife, I realized, did not take teasing well in any form and avoided it worse than the plague.

"No, sir," I said, and led the horses by the bridle down the sandy bank to the docking.

"Where you two going in the black of night anyway?" he asked.

"Up to Florence Junction for some peace and quiet."

He spat sideways and nodded as he walked beside me. "Be quieter up there than down here. A while ago they started shooting somewhere in town. Why, I'll bet the sun wasn't even down. Town ain't the same anymore. That Marshal Hendricks is a sore excuse for a lawman, and the sheriff we got ain't any better."

"Having lots of trouble?" I asked, stepping on the barge watching the horses closely as they came on the deck.

"Sure are. Why, that Hendricks can't even hit a stray dog."

"He has his shotgun tonight."

"That's what he missed with last time." The ferry man chuckled as he undid the mooring lines.

Stout took the other horse's bridle. "That's exactly my impression of him too," she said. "He won't capture those killers."

"Let him worry about those birds tonight. We'll be back at Sorrel's in a couple of hours."

She agreed and smiled back at me.

The ferry man was singing some sailing song as he

worked the hand winch that propelled the ferry across the river.

"You aren't worried, are you?" Stout asked.

"About what?"

"Well, I've never been married before, for one thing."

"Me either, silly. But we've got the rest of our lives to figure it out."

"Yes, we have. Thanks," she said softly.

The Gila River gently slapped the hollow-sounding side of the ferry and rushed off in a shiny flow to disappear into the ebony night. We stood at the bow, holding horses when we'd both rather have held each other.

On the north bank, after I paid the man, we disembarked and drove on. I trotted the horses rather than risk any breakneck speed in the darkness.

The jingle of harnesses, the deep-breathing horses, the plod of their hooves, and the singing wheels serenaded us. We pointed out constellations to each other and followed the North Star until the ghostly walls of the stage stop loomed before us and we drove through the gateway. A light shone on the depot porch in the center of the compound.

"*Señor,* I will put the horses up for you," one of Sorrel's employees said, taking charge of the team.

"Thank you," I said, and helped Stout off the rig.

"Well," I said.

"Well?" she asked.

"It must be a hundred steps to those rooms of ours."

"We using both of them?" she asked.

"I didn't figure on it. Did you?"

"Surprise!" someone shouted. The shrill whistle of a rocket went off. An ear-piercing scream split the night as it soared skyward in a trail of sparks and exploded in a great red burst.

Someone began playing a guitar and a trumpet joined in. Men and women were lighting Chinese lanterns strung all over. Sorrel and the Mexican woman Dolores came from the house all dressed up.

"You two did get married?" he asked. "Didn't you?"

We nodded, both dumbfounded.

"Come with me," the woman said to Stout. "I have a dress that will fit you for the party tonight." She led Stout away with Stout looking back at me for an answer. I shrugged, for I knew nothing about this surprise party they planned. Obviously the people that worked for Sorrel were going to celebrate our wedding.

"Come along," Sorrel said, "we will have a fiesta in you and your wife's honor. We needed a break. These Mexican people like to have an excuse to have some kind of celebration, and it isn't often there's a wedding. Who married you?"

"Father Nabors."

"Oh, the *padre*. You're Catholic?"

"No." I laughed as tables of food were set up. Children were dancing in the open yard.

"What if we hadn't come back tonight?" I asked.

"We would have partied with ourselves and then done it all again when you did come."

Sorrel poured some liquor in glasses for us. "Did it go well?"

"Not all of it. Those two outlaws we've been after

rode into Florence and recognized us coming out of the church. I figured we might not live to celebrate anything."

"Where did they go?"

"They rode off like the cowards they are. My gun was in the rig. Afterwards, we talked to Marshal Hendricks about them."

"A lot of good he'll do." Sorrel shook his head in disapproval of the man. "Here's to a long happy life for both of you. You'll be safe here."

I raised the glass and nodded in appreciation. The music was contagious and his liquor strong enough that I knew a little would do me. When Stout and Dolores returned, I must have blinked my eyes, for I hardly recognized my bride in the white blouse and dark skirt. Stout became a very lovely woman dressed in Dolores's clothing.

A great rocket went screaming off and this time burst into a blue cloud of sparkles as I took Stout in my arms and hugged her. She was crying.

"What's wrong?"

"I didn't expect this," she sobbed, meaning the fiesta and all the folks celebrating our wedding.

There was another aerial shot. This one was a yellow starburst and everyone oohed and aahed about it.

"You look great!" I said, and we began to dance.

Times like this were when my whole life went floating by in a dreamlike fashion. There was the first pony I ever rode, the day the young pretty teacher came to hold classes in our one-room schoolhouse, hiking through snowdrifts, hunting for rabbits, and hiding in the barn loft, playing summer games of hide-and-seek. Then I returned to the land of cactus and Spanish-speaking people, who each politely came by and wished the two of us well. It made a big knot in my throat. I knew that Stout was having the same trouble, sniffing in a handkerchief Dolores found for her. We danced together, then after a suitable time, we quietly excused ourselves to our room.

Dawn came with a rooster's crow. He sounded extra loud and proud as he crowed his head off.

"Should we go home today?" Stout asked from the bed.

I was looking out the small window at the courtyard. The Chinese lights were being taken down and the tables put away.

"What do you want to do?" I asked her.

"Sleep."

"We can do that."

She rose and stretched her arms over her head as she stood up. "Maybe after breakfast we can decide."

"Yes, we'll do that. I sort of like this married business. How about you?"

"It's fine. And it does save one of us from sleeping on the floor," she said with a mischievous grin.

I studied the courtyard while she dressed behind me. I figured I had my whole life to stare at her dressing anyway.

What should we do? Those two killers were still on the loose. Hendricks had probably done nothing about them.

"You're thinking about Dingus and Seawell, aren't you?" she asked, hugging me gently and burying her face in my back.

"I don't want them to ruin our honeymoon."

"We better get our saddle horses and find out where they went," she said, stepping back and sitting on the edge of the bed to pull on her boots. "You'll never feel right till those two are behind bars."

"You're right," I agreed. Still, my conscience kicked at me for putting their apprehension ahead of our life together.

In the main stage depot, Dolores served us fresh eggs and fried potatoes at the large table. Sorrel joined us.

"I never expected to see you two out so early," he said, taking a seat opposite us at the table.

Dolores gave him a disapproving elbow and poured his crockery mug full of strong black coffee. "You should watch what you say to people," the woman said to him sternly.

"Oh, Dolores, I'm just teasing." Sorrel tried to make her smile.

Dolores looked to the sky for God's help and left us.

"We've decided to keep looking for those two killers," I said.

"May I join you?" Sorrel asked. "I know this country well, and I think I could help if they resist."

"Can I ask why you want to go?"

Sorrel nodded. "You two are like the kids of my own I never had. I don't want to see anything happen to either of you. Besides, it gets boring running this stage stop."

I looked at Stout for an answer. He would be an asset. The man had more experience dealing with this kind than we did.

"Fine with me," she said quickly, and raised her cup to blow on it.

"Fine with me too. Where do we start?"

"Florence. I have sources there can tell us where they went or where they're staying."

"That's the way Locke does it," Stout said. "Goes in a saloon and comes out knowing the history of the place."

"It works, doesn't it?" I asked her.

"For you, yes, but not for my father. He goes in one and doesn't ever come out." Stout shook her head, and I imagined as a girl growing up she had lots of those experiences waiting out in front of saloons.

"We'll need to go to Globe and get our horses," I said.

"No, we have horses, saddles, and gear. I'll send one of the boys this morning to go get your horses and things. We can ride my horses and that'll save time."

Stout was busy thanking Dolores for the loan of her clothing. Sorrel and I left the two women talking to go saddle our mounts.

"Where can they go?" I asked as Sorrel caught a short, thick-set roan horse and led him over.

"Your wife'll like him," he said, giving me the lead. "Oh, south I guess, to Tucson or even Mexico. They might double back and go to New Mexico too."

"Marshal Tillman thought that, but instead they rode south into North Cut."

"When we find their trail, we'll be harder to shake than a burr in their tail." Sorrel laughed aloud. "See that Injun over there. That's Waggy. He's going along with us. He can track a lizard over those mountains."

"He ride a horse too?" I noticed he wore an unblocked dusty black hat with a feather in the band. His shirt was white cotton, and he wore a breechcloth with leather leggings. Waggy acted very disinterested in our horse-saddling business.

"No, but he can run all day. I think he's part jackrabbit."

"Wouldn't a horse be easier on him?"

Sorrel shook his head. "Trust me, Waggy will keep up and find the way they went."

The burly ex-buffalo-hunter Sorrel, an Indian tracker on foot, my wife and me—some posse we'd make. Somehow, I knew that with those two along, we certainly meant business. I felt better about our prospects of capturing the pair of killers than at any time before.

I mounted the dun Sorrel had picked for me and took the roan by the reins. Stout would be wondering about us. I needed to explain to her about Waggy too. The day was already heating up, and I knew we were in for a scorcher. Before we were through, North Cut's cool mountain air would be heaven to return to again. I sincerely hoped we could return there shortly.

CHAPTER
20

We drew some curious looks from townsfolk in Florence. Sorrel sat tall on the thick-set, short-legged chestnut horse he rode. He called it a mountain pony and raved on its ability in the Peraltas to be sure-footed and cover lots of rough terrain.

He reined to a stop in front of a saloon and told us to wait for him. Waggy stood in the shade of the building between the saloon and a store. I was amazed at the man's ability to match the horses' pace and not seem winded.

Stout searched around. "We must be something between a circus and a mirage because everyone in town has taken a hard look at us."

"Good," I said, standing up in the stirrups to abate some of my stiffness. "Maybe they've seen those other two as well."

Sorrel came out the swinging doors and shook his

head. "They never stopped in there. I also learned that if they are still in Florence, Hendricks didn't arrest them last night."

"Like we figured," I said aloud. Stout agreed with a hard nod and wry set to her lips. Our assumptions were correct about the 'huh?' asking lawman.

Stout reined her strawberry roan around, ready to go. Sorrel handily mounted his horse and motioned for us to ride south down the main street.

He said something I did not understand to Waggy. The Indian nodded and disappeared to the rear of the building.

"An Injun can learn more than a white man in a short while," Sorrel said as we rode three abreast down the street. The midmorning sun shone hot on the baked, hard-packed street. We shifted around the drays and wagons parked here and there.

"Hey, Sorrel!" a man on the sidewalk yelled. The big man guided his horse aside and leaned to listen. They spoke of a hay shipment for the stage horses. Stout and I waited discreetly a ways away.

"We're looking for two strangers," Sorrel finally said. "One is tall with a black beard, the other small and weasel-faced."

"I ain't sure, but they might be down in Dog Town. Two strangers about like that rode past me on the street headed there around dark last night."

I agreed with a nod, thinking that was after they'd shot at us. Good, they might still be in Florence. I saw Stout nod again in agreement. Strange how she and I could almost mentally telegraph things to each other.

I removed my hat and wiped my sweaty face on my sleeve as we prepared to move on.

"Dog Town is the Mexican part," Sorrel said. "Waggy will meet us there. He'll know if they're in Dog Town."

"Is it dangerous to go in there?" Stout asked.

"No, not if you're with me. Many of those people are relations to my workers." He smiled for her sake. "That's one reason why I came along."

"We're grateful," she said.

"No need. We can water our horses at the tank ahead. Waggy will come tell us what he knows in a little while."

I dismounted and loosened the cinch beside the wall with the lacy mesquites for thin shade. A tall adobe fence screened some property behind it. My curiosity was up about Sorrel's past since we had to wait.

"How did you ever get into buffalo hunting?" I asked.

"How did an educated man end up out there shooting and skinning buffalo is what you're asking?" Sorrel asked.

"Yes," I said, anxious for him to explain. "You're not illiterate nor, to my notion, the tough element I've met back home that earned a living doing that."

"In two years of shooting buffalo I banked over thirty thousand dollars. I married a Shoshone woman, we had a child, and I took them to live in the high country. The civilization I saw at the railheads was bawdy, dirty, and murderous. I wanted no part of it. We had more money than a sane man would spend in a lifetime. So she and I and the boy child went to the Rocky Mountains where eagles soar.

"Three white men found our cabin while I was gone hunting. They killed the boy, and after using my wife's body for their own purposes, they killed her." Sorrel looked across the street. His eyes were thin slits.

"Those dogs died as slow as she had. I ate their livers. Later I woke up from a very long drunk in Old Mexico. Some gentle people befriended me, and these people came north with me to find a place to live and raise their families. We built our fort in the forks of a dim road." Sorrel raised his head and looked at the returning lean runner.

"He knows something," Sorrel said, and greeted the man in Spanish. After he finished talking to his tracker, he turned to us. "They're at Martinez's," Waggy said. Sorrel pointed behind us.

"They may even be sleeping in a room there," Sorrel said. "The Martinez place is a sporting house."

"What do we do next?" My heart began to beat faster. I felt the pulse in my temples begin to race away. The twosome was finally close at hand.

"We ride into Dog Town," Sorrel said, then he turned to the Indian. "Waggy, you go down the alley."

"He has no gun," Stout said with a frown of concern as the man left at a trot.

"He'll be fine," Sorrel said, removing his high crown hat and speaking directly to Stout. "I know I cannot ask you to stay here. Where we are headed is not a place for a lady, but I've seen something in your look says you will not wait here."

"I'll do as my husband wishes me to do," Stout said. She rose in the stirrups, grasping the horn in her hand, and reseated herself as she waited for my word.

"She can ride with us. Stout dragged me out of Indian messes as serious or worse than this one can ever be."

"Your choice," Sorrel said, and swung up.

I tightened the cinch and remounted. We entered the narrow side street that wound like a snake. Empty carts partially blocked the street as diamond dark eyes of children peered at us, silenced from their play by our threatening presence. Burros slept hipshot; we had entered another world. Yellow curs snarled at first, but as we continued, they tucked their tails and whined, seeking cover as we rode by them.

On the porches, olive-skinned women looked curiously at us. Their dark eyes flashed as they wondered about our destination. I saw some of the women shake their heads and then tuck a basket under their arm to go on an errand.

My hand rested on the butt of my Colt, and I tried to see everything. The motion of a parrot in a large cage caught my eye in a threatening way. His jail hung under a porch roof.

"Who are you?" the green bird cried in English. "Well, who the devil are you?"

Sorrel twisted in the saddle and smiled for our sake. "He'd drive you crazy talking all day, wouldn't he?"

"Who are you? Who are you?" the bird squawked as we rode deeper into Dog Town.

I wondered if he knew. The street was lined with a small irrigation ditch that made a bend to the left. I saw two men come out of a business and mount their horses. For a moment my heart stopped.

It wasn't either of the pair we sought.

"Martinez's Cantina is still another block away," Sorrel said.

The high wall blocked our view when we dismounted. We hitched our horses. I looked for a moment at Stout wishing she would stay with the mounts, but I knew as she drew the Winchester out of the saddle scabbard she wouldn't remain behind.

"How many ways out?" she asked.

Sorrel told her there were only two ways out, this archway and the back way that Waggy guarded. Then he straightened to his full height of well over my six feet, and the three of us strode through the open gate.

Tables and chairs were scattered around the courtyard under the palm and crooked-trunk pepper trees. The loops of Chinese lanterns were strung overhead. I felt certain that fiesta time came here every day at dark.

I followed Sorrel's gaze to the second floor. Iron balconies dressed the french doors upstairs. We saw no one. Then, after I double-checked all the emptiness, Stout and I followed Sorrel into the saloon portion.

My eyes were slow to adjust to the darkness laden with the heavy perfume of sour beer, cigar smoke, and lavender toilet water. A young Mexican behind the bar rose up from polishing glasses. He did not act surprised to see three strangers in the barroom.

"We come for two gringos," Sorrel said. "One is tall, one is short."

Sorrel stood at the bar while he spoke to the man. Stout and I waited a respectable distance back to cover anything that might happen. I noticed a dusty mounted spotted lion of Mexico above the bar. It was a jaguar, a rare specimen this far north, I understood.

"Upstairs in rooms four and five," the bartender managed.

Sorrel thanked him and left a silver dollar on the bar. I wished he'd have let me do that. I nodded to Stout, and we followed Sorrel up the narrow stairs that his shoulders filled wall to wall.

At the head of the stairs he drew his Colt.

"Which room do you wish?" he asked.

"Four," I said.

"We'll kick open the doors at the same time," Sorrel said under his breath. "Use your heel right at the knob, and first thing you shoot a hole in the ceiling that will disorient them. Then order them to surrender."

I didn't need to ask anymore. The wooden door was less than ten steps from me. First, I positioned Stout at the head of the stairs where she would be out of the line of fire and also able to cover any possible threat from downstairs. Then I stepped to the door and listened. There was some low talking inside I could not make out. I wondered what doings I'd interrupt. Sorrel was in position.

"Now!" he shouted. The door gave way like a rotten rail, and the gunshots hurt my ears. The resulting cloud of smoke and plaster dust nearly obscured the room and its contents. A screaming, near naked woman ran out by me to escape.

"Get your hands high or get ready to die!"

Mink Seawell stood up in his dirty underwear with his shaking hands over his head. "Don't shoot!"

"Tell me something then. Badger Jones, the cowboy you killed on the Flagstaff road. Tell me how he died."

"I-I-I don't know."

I crossed the room in a rage. I grapped a fistful of his underwear and shoved the gun in his belly with force enough to drive some of the wind out of him.

"I ain't listening to your lies. Either you start talking or I'm spilling your blood on this floor." The words came from between my clenched teeth, and I fully intended to blow his rotten guts out.

"We killed him for his money!" Mink screamed in a high-pitched desperate voice. "Dingus shot him, I swear! Not me! Not me!"

Filled with contempt, I pushed the outlaw toward the door. My eyes burned from the gunsmoke. I knew in another minute I'd kill Seawell and be no better than the likes of them. Sorrel stood guarding the bearded Dingus in the hall.

"Get against the wall," Sorrel ordered. "Put your hands high and spread your legs out."

"What you going to do to us?" Mink pleaded.

"Blow your head off," Sorrel said, "if you don't do as I say."

"They can't do that, can they, Dingus?"

"Shut up! You done said enough to get us hung now," Dingus told his partner.

"Go get the short one's clothes and then check both rooms; they may have evidence the law will need. I'll hold them here."

"Sorry, ma'am," Sorrel said to Stout. "They ain't exactly dressed proper."

"That's all right," she said, holding the Winchester level on them. "They aren't getting away this time either."

"No, ma'am, they aren't going to do that."

I rushed out with his clothing and tossed it to Seawell to dress. "Are you all right?" I asked her.

"I'm fine." She beamed.

"Good. We'll be out of here in a minute. Soon as I get the rest of their things." I started to turn, then I stepped back to tell her. "Did you hear Seawell admit that they killed Badger Jones?"

She nodded her head with tight lips.

It was over.

The return trip required four days to retrace our way back to the North Cut. One night was spent having another fiesta with Sorrel and his people at the junction. The next night, Skyler's stage line rented the honeymoon suite for us in the Globe's Grand Hotel and, in addition, they paid us the two hundred dollars reward.

Mr. Kincaid let us sleep in his hay shed. Late afternoon on the fourth day, with the cool mountain breeze in our faces, we were gratefully looking down at Linter's store.

"I think Tate and Erv are down there." She pointed to some horses. I read the excitement on her face.

"You going to tell them we're married or do I?" I asked, enjoying her discomfort at the prospect.

Something in the pens caught my eye. It was a light-colored horse. As we rode closer I pointed him out to Stout, and she nodded. "That's your gold horse down there."

"I think so too. Look at him, they sure didn't break his spirit." Her eyes were afire with excitement as we set spurs to our horses in a race for the store.

"Look, it's them! Stout and Locke!" Tate shouted. The two sisters ran out to greet us. Carl Linter even half ran to hug Stout and shake my hand.

"Tell us. Tell us what happened." Tate said, unable to stand the suspense.

Stout pulled off her glove and showed them the gold ring. The showing drew a deep hush.

"The killers are in jail, and we were married in Florence five days ago, best I can count," Stout said, shaking her head in a daze.

"Oh, that's super!" The sisters shrieked and yelled in excitement, hugging and pounding poor Stout. "Wonderful! Great!"

I had other plans. The lariat in my hand, I headed for the corral.

"Alkie Tie brought him here a couple days ago," Carl said, hurrying to keep up with me. "I paid him forty bucks for the horse. That was what you said to do."

"You did fine. I'll pay you as soon as I rope him."

"Sure," Carl said.

I looked back at the three sisters. Each one was talking at the same time as they came in a cluster toward the pens. I climbed over the rails and fed out the loop as the yellow horse raced around with his flaxen mane flagging. He circled me.

With the lariat in my right hand, I worked the loop large enough and the horse doubled his speed as I let him go around me. Then I threw it. The circle settled over his pin ears and around his neck. I jerked the slack hard with my right hand and set my heels in the dirt. The rope training settled the big horse. He braked and snorted freely as he came back to me.

"Damn! Brother-in-law, you did that like a real ranch hand," Tate said, hugging the top rail of the corral. "You must have really been practicing a lot lately."

I shook my head. "No, but I'm going to be a rancher around here. My teacher said I had a lot to learn."

Stout was looking at me over the rail with that mischievous smile and shaking her head. "You may make that grade yet, Locke McTavish."

"I hope so," I said, petting the gold horse on the nose and studying the blue-green mountain rim above North Cut. At least no one laughed at me this time when I said I'd become a rancher.